FAVORITE MONSTER

FAVORITE MONSTER

stories by
SHARMA SHIELDS

Autumn House Press

PITTSBURGH

Autumn House Press Staff
Editor-in-Chief and Founder: Michael Simms
Managing Editor: Adrienne Block
Co-Founder: Eva-Maria Simms
Community Outreach Director: Michael Wurster
Fiction Editors: Sharon Dilworth, John Fried
Assistant Editor: Emily Cerrone
Associate Editor: Giuliana Certo
Media Consultant: Jan Beatty
Publishing Consultant: Peter Oresick
Tech Crew Chief: Michael Milberger
Intern: Alecia Dean

PENNSYLVANIA
COUNCIL
ON THE
Autumn House Press receives state arts funding support through
a grant from the Pennsylvania Council on the Arts, a state agency
funded by the Commonwealth of Pennsylvania, and the National
Endowment for the Arts, a federal agency.

ISBN: 978-1-932870-58-9
Library of Congress Control Number: 2011938982

ACKNOWLEDGMENTS

"The McGugle Account" appeared in *Iowa Review*
"Field Guide to Monsters of the Inland Northwest" appeared in
Kenyon Review
"Lying Down" appeared in *Sonora Review*
"Sunshine and the Predator" appeared in *Hawai'i Review*
"Souvenirs" appeared in *Fugue*
"Antropolis" appeared in *Primavera*
"The Tylenol Cheerleader" appeared online in *Monkey Bicycle*
"Morsels" appeared online in *Memorious*

In regards to the making of this book, thank you to the following:
the MFA program at the University of Montana; Autumn House Press;
Adrienne Block; Stewart O'Nan; Artist Trust; the Spokane County Library
District; J. Robert Lennon, Jess Walter, Aryn Kyle and Diana Spechler; my
friends and family; my parents for their unconditional support; my brother,
John Paul Shields, and my close friend, Elizabeth Roewe, for their instrumental advice regarding the final draft of this manuscript; my beautiful
son, Henry; and most importantly, my husband, Sam, for his editorial input
and for his unyielding faith in my work.

This manuscript could not have been completed without a generous grant from Artist Trust of Washington State: www.artisttrust.org

CONTENTS

vvvvvvvvvvvvvvvvvvvvvvvvv

THE McGUGLE ACCOUNT

ʌʌʌʌʌʌʌʌʌʌʌʌʌʌʌʌʌʌʌʌʌʌʌʌʌ

We were all surprised when Brian hired the Cyclops. His references only spoke Greek. His sole job experience was shepherding. It was uncertain if he could commit to two years. No matter. Brian saw something formidable in him. He had followed a similar hunch when he hired me. Despite my lack of PR experience, and despite my nervous stutter during the interview, I had become one of our company's top performers.

I was speaking on my headset to a client when I saw the Cyclops for the first time. From my cramped cubicle I admired his backside as he exited Brian's office. I've always been attracted to tall men with broad shoulders, and given my collegiate foray into the punk scene, I didn't even blink at the tiny green sprig of hair that sat like a piece of unmown lawn atop his head. No, it wasn't until he turned that I saw why others described him as revolting: the large eye, settled like a rough diamond above his eyebrows (not under them, as many would think) was, to put it mildly, intimidating. But what an eye it was! The color of warm sand, bright and penetrating. So penetrating that when he caught my gaze I swore he could see the color of my bones beneath my expensive tweed suit and inexpensive (and somewhat gritty) bra and underwear. And that voice! I heard him now, as he spoke to Brian, and I stopped talking in mid-sentence to Mrs. Lipman so that I could eavesdrop more effectively.

I had barely begun to enjoy the Cyclops' melodic enthusiasm about working with our company when my client, Mrs. Lipman, began chirping in my right ear. After her tedious public involvement with crank and the home shopping network, she hungered for as much counsel as she could get. "Hello, Carol?" Mrs. Lipman said. "Can you hear me? You're speaking on your headset again, aren't you, Carol. I've asked you repeatedly not to use your headset. It makes you sound like some robot from distant space. Can you hear me, Carol? You were saying something about my choice of tortillas, correct? About choosing the tortillas with the pink ribbon? The breast cancer tortillas? Instead of the white cheapies?"

"An analogy, Mrs. Lipman," I said. "My point is that for someone so famous, the smallest choices you make will influence the media's opinion of you." She marveled over this statement, saying "Yes, I see," pleased as she

1

always was with any grandiose platitude. Around me, chairs scraped back and polite laughter ballooned. Brian was introducing the Cyclops around the office. I told Mrs. Lipman I would call her back and hung up.

Brian and the Cyclops approached my desk, smiling broadly. I stood and extended my hand. Like prairie dogs risen from their earthen holes, the heads of my colleagues bobbed above the cubicle walls, their expressions less curious than bored.

With a sense of wonderment I allowed the Cyclops' hand to swallow up my own. "It's a delight to meet you, Ms. Horne," he said. "Brian was raving about your work here."

So soft, his voice, as though it could lull you to sleep. He was very well-spoken for a Cyclops.

I told this to my colleague Kent later that day. Kent grunted and rolled his eyes.

"More proof of Brian's incompetence," Kent said. His gelled hair sat stiffly on his head like the shining blade of a guillotine. "He's obviously a monster. Did you smell him?"

"Like cooked garbage," an intern agreed.

"I thought he was nice," I said. We were standing around the fax machine, five or six of us, waiting for our faxes to crawl out of the machine's unsmiling mouth.

"'Nice' is the adjective people use when they don't have something better to say," Kent intoned. Then he sang loudly, "Carol's found a new boyfriend."

My coworkers laughed. "Yeah, right," I said with feigned playfulness. "I mean, come on, he's totally gross. Really, he's disgusting."

But truthfully, I didn't find the Cyclops gross or disgusting. Aside from the large club he always carried ("For wolves or worse," he told me), and despite the smell of livestock that trailed him everywhere, he was far more refined and thoughtful than the other men in the office. His pants – while faintly stained – were always neatly pressed. He could quote entire poems of Yeats and Sappho. Even more impressive was that he always asked everyone, no matter how busy he was, how his or her day was going. Clients perceived his incongruity as a sign of superiority and began requesting his services. To my delight, we were teamed up on a new project together, and after a few engaging weeks I complimented him on his impressive vocabulary and grammar.

"I read a lot of books in the field," the Cyclops explained. He meant field literally, as in the field where he shepherded goats. I pictured him lolling on a vast green hillside, his feet and chest bare, holding a hardcover book above his face at just the right angle to block the hot Mediterranean sun.

"Any favorites?" I asked. I had been a literature major in college and in my rare haughty moments fancied myself a scholar.

"Of our contemporaries I enjoy Cormac McCarthy. I like tales of war and death. But the authors I forever return to are long perished: Tolstoy, Homer, Proust. Have you ever read Proust?"

Proust was one of those authors I wanted desperately to read but knew I never would. I had been assigned a few chapters in college that I completely blew off for a week of reality television. For much of my life I wore my unfamiliarity with Proust like a red cloak of literary shame. The fact that even this spelunking Cyclops had read Proust was a bit humiliating.

"Proust," I said. "Yes, of course."

The Cyclops smiled at me, displaying the crooked gray kernels of his teeth. "I like you, Carol," he said. "You don't seem like the type that would work in a PR firm."

"Neither do you," I told him. This time I wasn't lying.

Why lie about Proust? Even as I was telling the lie some part of my brain was screaming at me, *Don't lie you idiot, you won't be judged for it!* But I had a severe problem with wanting to please people. Especially people I liked. Like Brian, my boss. Or the Cyclops. Or Amanda Davenport in grade school, whose hair was always smooth and shining and who could always color perfectly within the lines. I told her that I, too, used to be a coloring expert, but after a debilitating car wreck that shattered my wrists (and scorched my hair, making it frizzy), it was all I could do to stay on the page. Amanda informed the teacher and the teacher called my mom and that night I had to lean against the cold bathroom sink for five minutes with a bar of soap in my mouth. This did not keep me from lying again, although it did make me more careful about the magnitude of lie. I shied away from the larger deceits and began living in a white smoke of smaller half-truths. So it was when I lied to the Cyclops about Proust. And it was admittedly gratifying when he beamed back at me. I could see my watery reflection projected affectionately in his enormous brown-flecked eye. But as ever when I lied, the gnawing disappointment in myself, and the gnawing feeling that I was about to get caught, diminished the magnitude of my triumph. I smiled back at him half-heartedly.

A few days later the McGugle Account was created. The Cyclops and I were assigned to the same team. I was typically the Go-To Girl in such situations, but the McGugle Corporation had fallen into near disrepair. The youngest McGugle son was in court, defending himself from three sexual harassment accusations. The McGugle trophy wife was an admitted coke-head and alcoholic. While on a wine-tasting tour of the Yakima Valley, she drove her car through the brick wall of a winery's tasting room. Mr. McGugle, himself, was rumored to be the most avid patron of a high-class escort ring. It was a big company and a bigger mess.

"You mortals," the Cyclops muttered with a woeful shake of his head. We were eating pizza slices in the office near midnight. We were trying to find a positive light in all of this. "No matter what you have, it's never enough."

Kent found this remark offensive. "What about you? You were a shepherd. Wasn't that a blissful enough existence? It's not like you were recruited here, you know."

Some of my colleagues snorted. Earlier, the Cyclops had shoveled down an entire goat cheese pizza while the hungry interns glowered at him. They had shuffled in their chairs and muttered angrily to one another but avoided any direct invective. The Cyclops' large spiked club lay casually on the table near his Blackberry and the interns eyed it uneasily.

"For your information," the Cyclops said tersely, "my goats died." He had pizza sauce on his earlobe. He started to say something else but then stopped.

"What," the boldest of the interns responded, "did you eat them?"

The Cyclops' face reddened.

"We're getting off task," I said loudly. "Let's please turn our attention back to the press release. I personally enjoy the idea of a McGugle Bazaar. Anyone else?"

As the team began their vociferous opining, I caught the Cyclops' eye and touched my earlobe carefully. His eye widened. He reached up with his giant hairy hand to remove the sauce from his ear. It smeared onto his fingers like blood. He gazed back at me gratefully. I considered winking but abstained, as I assumed such an innocuous gesture could be offensive to any creature possessing only one eye.

An hour later the Cyclops escorted me to my car. He held his club menacingly and commented that a young beautiful woman should not be walking alone so late at night. I blushed. "Thirty-five is not so young," I told him.

"You're a mere girl in Cyclops years."

We reached my car. I jangled my keys. "Well," I said. "Thank you."

"No, thank you." His eye was staring down at me mushily. I was nervous that he would try to kiss me right then and there in the parking lot, where one of my colleagues might find us.

Instead he leaned against his club and looked up at the stars. "'Desire makes everything bloom,'" he said wistfully.

"What?"

The Cyclops looked down at me again. "Don't you remember? Proust?"

For lack of an answer, I dropped my keys. I stooped to pick them up, and so did the Cyclops, and his forehead hit the back of my head so hard that I dropped to the ground. Yellow blotches swarmed like bees in my vision.

"Oh dear," he said. "That smarts, I'll bet." He helped me to my feet. In the lamplight, his face was wretched and scarred and now twisted with worry.

"I'm alright," I said, brushing his hands away. My ears rang and my head ached. "I'm alright."

I got in my car. He rapped on the window with his acorn-sized knuckles. I rolled the window down and looked up at him, smiling nervously.

"I'm sorry about your head," he said softly.

"I know. It's okay. It was an accident."

"I really meant it when I said thank you."

I smoothed my skirt under my thighs and then poked the key into the ignition.

"You haven't read Proust," he said suddenly, folding his wide hairy fingers over the door. It was not a question. I sat back in surprise, my hands dropping into my lap. "I knew it."

His voice was gentle, forgiving. Something like a large flower opened sadly within me. "I didn't mean to lie," I said, even though that was a lie, too. I wanted to recline in the front seat and go to sleep.

The Cyclops cleared his throat. "'Lies are essential to humanity. They are perhaps as important as the pursuit of pleasure and moreover are dictated by that pursuit.'" He crouched down next to me as he spoke, his big head hanging like a rough pale planet in the window.

"Proust again?" I said. He nodded and reached for me. He pressed his big lips onto mine. I was surprised at how gentle and sweet he was, quite the opposite of what you would expect from one so big and rough. I opened my eyes to find his wide high eye staring absently over my hairline. He released me and invited me to his cave.

Despite my rattling heart I managed to say, "Should I drive?"

The Cyclops squeezed into my car by reclining the passenger seat down flat and lying prone, giving directions to his cave via the stars he read through the open sunroof. I was too nervous to speak now. I glanced at his enormous Grecian thighs in his khakis (where did he buy those, I wondered) and worried if making love to a Cyclops was even technically possible. These were frightening thoughts, but then he reached over and with his large hand stroked my hair, and the sweetness of this gesture soothed me. I was under a spell. When instructed I turned the steering wheel obediently, forgetting the blinker. When he spoke I listened with all of my heart. When we reached his cave half the night had passed and the spindly moon had already set, but to me, content in my lustful suffering, the drive had been a mere pinprick in the vast open wound of time.

We were somewhere far from Seattle. Eastern Washington, I assumed, in a land of rolling hills and no trees. Machines had carved enormous circles into the farmland so that they resembled landing platforms for visiting spaceships. We were on top of the highest butte in sight, looking out over the smaller hills that undulated like a frozen ocean into the dark horizon. The night was clear; the wind was fierce. My hair was whipped into my eyes as I stepped from the car, and the stinging strands were momentarily blinding. One of my high heels broke. I did not complain. I merely slipped off my shoes and trod on the cool dirt toward the rocky outcropping where the Cyclops stood waiting for me. He motioned for me to go ahead of him. I walked with feigned bravery between two large boulders and into the hillside. The smell was very strong, farm animals and grain. I couldn't see anything in the inky blackness.

"Here we go," the Cyclops said, striking a match. A fire exploded into light and the room flickered into view. The high ceilings were domed nicely overhead and the rock walls were lined with large attractively painted jugs.

"Wine," he grunted, uncorking a jug and pressing it to his mouth. The wine dribbled down his chin and onto his Ralph Lauren polo.

He passed the wine jug to me. I wasn't strong enough to grip it, so he gingerly brought it to my lips. It was delicious. The taste helped to lessen the fecund animal smell emanating from the corner, where a pen of three goats bleated incessantly for their dinner.

"These are my children," the Cyclops boasted cheerfully. "Well, not really of course, but I care for them like they are." He told me their names in Greek, but I only caught the name of Hector, a small gray goat with dull yellow horns. "I'm building up my flock again. Three is an okay start, but I'd like to have nineteen or more. Nearby there is a ranch with a dozen or so good goats. I'll hopefully have them by Friday of next week."

"How much do they cost?" I asked, genuinely curious.

The Cyclops waved his club through the air and laughed. "Gratis," he said. He set the club down next to a pile of straw that must have been his bed. After one last chuckle he grew solemn. We watched one another seriously for several moments and for once I was strong enough to look him squarely in the eye without turning away. "Come here," he said, unbuckling his belt, and I came.

Later, lying in the dark on the straw that was stabbing me relentlessly wherever I turned, feeling pleasantly bruised and pawed from the night before, I began wondering if I should escape. Blind him with a hot poker, maybe, and then flee clinging to the belly of one of his goats. The thought made me smile in the dark, because the goats were so small and smelly that I couldn't imagine their being an effective hiding place. More realistically, I could leave a note. Tiptoe to my car and drive the five hours back to Seattle with my broken shoe in the passenger seat. This was my modus operandi in those days – initial excitement about becoming involved with someone, followed by an adrenaline-packed flight response that I assumed would protect me from future awkwardness and pain, whether my awkwardness and pain or the other person's, I was never sure. Somehow I understood that the Cyclops deserved better, but I questioned my motives. Despite his being smarter, kinder and sweeter than most, and despite his being well-endowed (though not, fortunately, to the point where our coupling had been a disaster), I began wondering if I was confusing lust and pity. Maybe I was feeling sorry for him, for having to go through life as the freak, as the weirdo. I pictured us walking down the street together, him looming over me, the crowds parting before us, their faces twisted with curiosity and fear. I pictured the interns at our wedding ceremony, making farting sounds in the back rows and doubling over with laughter. The Cyclops gave a loud snore then, an earth-splitting snore, and even one of the goats bleated in fear.

I lingered. Faint light began filtering into the cave. The Cyclops snored on. I turned to gaze at him and was shocked by his ugliness. The deep craters on his face (scars from Cycloptic acne?) and the bulbous eye wiggling beneath the fabric of his eyelid were newly hideous to me, and I chided myself for being so cruel. What fairy tale had I presumed would happen? That I would sleep with him and then find upon awakening that he had transformed? That he was a two-eyed handsome prince? That his

7

dungy cave was an alabaster castle? That I was an honest person finding love and beauty in the monstrous?

This last part might have become true. But when the Cyclops awoke I was already buttoning my dress and shaking out my hair.

"Wait," the Cyclops protested, rising to his feet and brushing the straw away from his powerful figure. "I can make breakfast." He wrapped a loincloth around his waist and I realized that this was his version of hanging around the house in boxers. It was almost charming if I wasn't already feeling so pale and sick.

"I'll call you," I said. It came out coldly.

The Cyclops' eye flickered. In it there floated a flotsam of hurt. "Yeah right," he said, and it was the only time I heard him be sarcastic. "I'll bet."

He walked me to the cave entrance. In the morning light, he was terrifying. I let him kiss me on the forehead. Once settled in my car, I breathed an enormous sigh of relief.

The following Monday we were all surprised to hear that the Cyclops had been fired. Brian called me into his office, distressed. Only the day before the Cyclops had slaughtered the entire McGugle clan during an unscheduled meeting at their hotel. He had taken their carcasses back to his cave near Pullman and had cooked them over a spit. He ate most of them and then deposited their remains in a cornfield. He had called Brian that very morning to confess and apologize.

"I liked the old guy," Brian said, wiping his nose. "True, he smelled horribly. Like a morgue. And his face was hideous. But what confidence! Really, a creative genius. Nonetheless, it's impossible to keep him on staff after what he did. Reprehensible, really. I doubt I'll even give him a letter of reference. As for you, Carol, we'll need you to write copy for a new hire. I'd like to post it online today."

"Where – where is he now?" My stomach had pierced the soles of my feet, and I stood there stupidly in its mucky glue.

"Gone, I guess," Brian shrugged. "The authorities wanted to speak with him but he was long gone – his goats, too. My guess is he returned to his homeland, where this sort of behavior is more acceptable."

I moved into the hallway numbly. It was not that I was in love. I wasn't. Love wasn't realistic. Love raised too many worrisome questions. For example: Would our children have three eyes? Would my hips be wide enough for their delivery? Would they have pale shocks of green ear hair? What would my mother say? But I kept thinking of his lips and the softness of his voice, and I wondered when it was, exactly, that my lying had become so deeply entrenched that I was now lying exclusively to myself.

My colleagues threw a work party in honor of the Cyclops' departure. One of the interns baked cupcakes. "So long to the armpits of death," Kent said, tearing into a bag of chips. The interns guffawed over their cokes. I was silent. I sat in my cubicle, perusing the new resumes that were pouring in by the dozens. While a few prospects seemed promising, especially a Ms. Scylla, a successful head-hunter with specific maritime experience, none of them seemed lovable.

A year later I received a red crate from some remote Mediterranean island. It arrived at work. I asked Kent to help me lift it into my car. "Can't," he said, pointing to his shoulder. "Racquetball." The interns helped me instead. After dragging it into my house, I left it unopened for several weeks. Finally, during a gray rain that left me bored and depressed, I uncorked a jug of ouzo and sat on the straw pile in the corner of my bedroom. With a loud sigh I braced myself before attacking the crate with my hammer. I clawed through a cheerful cloud of cotton balls until my fingertips collided with the hard covers of several books. I pulled them out one by one. Marcel Proust. His collected works. They were frustratingly all in French. A small card – no name attached – fluttered from the guts of the largest volume. A Proust quote, in English:

"'There is no man, however wise, who has not at some period of his youth said things, or lived in a way the consciousness of which is so unpleasant to him in later life that he would gladly, if he could, expunge it from his memory.'"

Gladness returned to me then. Someone somewhere understood me and suffered as I did.

Whenever I begin to doubt myself, as I invariably do, and wish in terror that I had not turned out the way that I have, I open up these strange, dusty, illegible books and I reread this note. Then all seems benign again, at least temporarily, like there is a great eye penetrating my lies and observing the goodness within me.

VVVVVVVVVVVVVVVVVVVVVVVVVV

THE CHIRP OF THE CRICKET

ΛΛΛΛΛΛΛΛΛΛΛΛΛΛΛΛΛΛΛΛΛΛΛΛΛ

Last year my husband began to shrink.

Roy noticed it first. For a week or so, he merely observed the change, expecting the loss to reverse itself, but each day upon awakening he found himself further reduced. Despite the swiftness of this process, I was completely unaware of it until one evening when I made a simple request of Roy that he could not fulfill. I was cooking for us as I always did, preparing a Spanish omelet. There was an unopened jar of olives sitting on the top shelf of the cupboard, too distant for me to reach. Roy, at his normal height, could reach the shelf easily, without even rising onto his toes.

"Roy," I said, pointing. "Olives."

After thirty years of marriage, there was no need to use silly words like *please* or *could you.*

Roy stood behind me, leaning against the kitchen island, reading an article from a restoration magazine. He had recently retired from his job as a general contractor, a reluctant retirement at best, but he had found himself tiring too easily at work, growing bored as he listened to his clientele and their lofty and often misplaced desires for their homes. I had accepted the news of his retirement eagerly, looking forward to having more time with him, but once it was realized, I grew somewhat irritable, now finding him perennially underfoot. I was reminded of my children when they were young, how they needed constant entertainment and care, how tuning them out for even a moment resulted in a high, ceaseless whine. Roy did not sound his whine audibly, of course. After all, he was a grown man. But I could hear it just the same when I walked by him, doing my daily dusting of the shelves or ferrying the laundry to and from the utility room. He would stare up at me with those petulant beady eyes as though begging me to guide him somewhere meaningful. It was, needless to say, an awkward adjustment.

With a little time, however, we grew accustomed to our new lifestyle. Roy found ways to entertain himself – magazines, gardening, tiny improvements on our home that I agreed to only if he stayed out of my way – and I learned to tune him out while completing my daily tasks as a housewife. I also took up the habit of delegating small duties to him, hoping to make him feel as useful and essential to our household as I was. Retrieving the jar of olives was one such thing. Truthfully, I hadn't kept objects on the top shelf for years. But now I did, so that Roy could fetch them for me. It was part of my grand strategy to interrupt his boredom. And it seemed successful.

Now I stood before the smoking skillet, poking at the eggs with a wooden spoon, awaiting a jar of olives that never came. I turned to find him standing before the cupboard, staring up at it with a quizzical look on his face, as though he were staring into the belly of an alien spacecraft. His sleepy look of confusion annoyed me. If I had stopped for a moment and considered him more closely, I might have noticed how much shorter he was, standing there before the familiar cabinets, but instead I mistook my husband's inability for laziness, and I stiffened.

Gripping the wooden spoon like a shiv, I repeated hotly, "Roy. Get me the olives."

Roy knew better than to disobey. He stood on his tiptoes and grunted, stretching for all he was worth. His pink fingers scrabbled at the air.

I stared at him, alarmed. "Stop it," I said. "Stop joking around."

Roy fell back onto the soles of his feet and sighed. "I can't reach it anymore, Anna. I've shrunk. I'll need a step stool. A chair. Something."

"Impossible," I said. I pointed out that he had retrieved a canister of breadcrumbs from these same shelves only the week before. "People don't shrink in the course of a day or two," I added.

"I've lost almost three inches," Roy complained. "Look." He pulled at his pant legs. "My clothes are too big."

It was true – his pant cuffs dragged along my tile floor. He had rolled up his shirtsleeves so that the fabric bunched around his strangely delicate wrists.

"Should I call the doctor?" he pressed.

I considered this. In my opinion, it was still too early to panic. Probably he was suffering from a minor illness. Arthritis, I thought, or maybe simple exhaustion. I gave him a peck on the cheek, tapping him lightly on the shoulder with my wooden spoon. It left a greasy imprint on his shirt, like a kiss from a vampire.

"Let's just wait. A little loss of height is no concern, really. We are aging, after all."

Roy nodded, relieved. As long as I was unconcerned, all was well. It was typical in our relationship that I led and he followed. And so I chose for us to remain upbeat. As for the olives, Roy dragged in a chair from the dining room and stood on it to retrieve the jar. The dinner was delicious, but I found myself considering the new shape of Roy's head, which seemed oddly deflated, like a helium balloon that had been sitting out too long in the sun.

Roy's condition worsened. One afternoon, as we grappled beside one another in the foyer, hanging our coats and scarves after a brisk walk, I realized with a start that my husband and I stood eye to eye. I was not, by any means, a short woman, but when we were married, Roy had towered over me by nearly a foot. I gave a gasp of fright.

Roy said, blanching, "It's undeniable now, isn't it?"

I admitted, as calmly as I could, that it did not look good.

Roy was very grim. He suspected that something was terribly wrong with him. I told him "Nonsense," but went into the den immediately to phone the physician. The receptionist told me that they were booked solid for several weeks, but I was extraordinarily persuasive, almost to the point of cruelty. She buckled, booking us for the following morning.

The physician's office was very warm. I sweated lightly but did not take off my coat. I was hoping for a quick, easy visit. An instant cure.

The physician muttered over my husband's charts. He measured Roy's height and compared his findings. Nonplussed, he fell into a deafening silence, rubbing at a small blue vein throbbing near his temple.

Finally, grasping, the doctor asked, "Has there been any change in your diet?"

My husband said no, but I countered with some urgency, "Why, yes. There has been. We've begun eating dried fruits. I brought home some dried peaches the other day. We've been devouring them like crazy."

The doctor considered this. I realized with a flutter of hope that my husband looked a bit like a dried fruit, himself, desiccated and shrunken. I pointed this out to the doctor and he studied Roy carefully, nodding.

"Probably the dried fruit," he said with a refreshing confidence. Then he frowned in concentration, drawing from his breast pocket a prescription pad and a pen. "Fresh fruit from now on. And more water. To counter the dehydration. I'm also writing you a prescription for a steroid. Let's see if we can't try beefing you up again."

On the way home from the drug store, prescription in hand, we bubbled over with excited chatter, sure that we had found the culprit. The dried fruit, I asserted. Dehydration, Roy agreed. I threw out all of the dried fruit in the cupboards. Roy quaffed giant brimming glasses of cold water.

"I'm cured," he told me. "I can feel it." He was sure that he had not shrunk an inch since the doctor's appointment. In fact, he sensed that he was growing taller. The steroids were clearly working: he seemed stronger, fuller in the shoulders and legs. His hair was thicker, darker. We celebrated with wine at dinner. He was relieved, and I tried to be, too, but I couldn't help but notice that his chin was barely floating over the surface of the table. A little shorter and he would need a booster seat. I kept my thoughts to myself, hoping that his positive thinking would help the reversal along.

A few days passed, however, and, emerging from the garage late one afternoon, Roy reported that he could no longer reach the gas pedal. I took him to the department store to buy him some new clothes, as I had already hemmed and re-hemmed his pants beyond repair. The woman in the children's department eyeballed us with apprehension. We pretended that we were shopping for our grandchildren. Despite our bluff, it was obvious that the pants were for poor Roy. We returned to the physician again and, troubled, he sent us to a specialist.

The specialist took a great interest in my husband but admitted that he was just as flummoxed as we were.

"I'm beginning to think," he told us, "that this is psychosomatic."

He instructed Roy to quit the steroids. He wondered aloud if my husband weren't severely depressed.

I regarded my husband blandly, expecting him to deny any such silliness. He did not, however, appear surprised by the question.

"Depressed," he said dully. "Yes. Yes, perhaps a little."

He gave a nervous glance in my direction. I leaned forward in my seat, clacking my heels against the floor, my mouth hanging open.

"Perhaps," he continued slowly, dragging his eyes away from mine and locking them onto the golden latch of the heavy office door, "perhaps more than a little."

The specialist gave us the phone number of a renowned therapist, as well as the phone number for a second specialist, so that we could immediately seek out another opinion. Roy pumped the specialist's hand as we left, thanking him in a manner that I personally found effusive.

"What are you so grateful for?" I demanded as we walked to the car. "That quack thinks you're suffering from psychosis."

"Depression," Roy corrected, opening up the driver's side door for me.

The door dwarfed him. He grunted a little as he pulled. I settled myself into the driver's seat and violently stabbed the key into the ignition.

Roy clambered into his own seat with another groan of effort.

A bell sounded in my ears, an incessant pounding gong. I drove recklessly, taking turns too fast, refusing to stop at crosswalks. A mother, standing there on the sidewalk with her two small children, gave me the bird as we passed. I pressed down on the accelerator, imagining my foot pressing into the skull of that wretched specialist.

"But do you really," I finally exploded as we crossed from the town into the open countryside, "think that you're depressed? You haven't been depressed in your entire life, Roy."

"It's very likely," Roy answered, strangely. "I think about our children, so far away from us now, and I think about my old job, and how I miss it. About a month ago I was so bored, or so upset, I'm not sure, that I just took to screaming at the top of my lungs."

"Screaming?"

"You were away, of course. At the grocery store." Roy's feet dangled far above the pristine floor mat. "I just marched around the house, screaming bloody murder. When I finally shut up – it must have been after fifteen minutes – I experienced a great peace."

"Good God," I said. "Imagine what the neighbors might think."

"I don't," he said.

"What?"

"I don't imagine. I don't care. I've done it repeatedly now, Anna. It seems," he groped for a word here, "cathartic."

In all of our years together my husband had never spoken to me in such a way. In his words hummed a violent defiance. My fingers quaked against the steering wheel. It was difficult to concentrate on the road. Indeed a vision flashed before me of driving us headlong into the great oak at the end of our street. *If only to end this miserable conversation.* I considered our tidy, well-dressed home, filling up like a balloon with the poisonous gas of my husband's screams. It made me sick to learn that I had been unwittingly inhaling these screams for weeks now.

Roy had always been too habitual for secrets. Our own children often complained about his lack of a sense of adventure, of his routine-driven life – a life I kept perfectly manicured for him, precisely because he required it of me. Our children kept their own secrets from him simply because, as they said, he wouldn't understand. How frequently I sat with my daughters and sons as they whispered, "Don't tell Dad," and I nodded eagerly, vindicated by their trust. Of course, I did always tell Roy. I kept nothing from him. Even my anger I shared unhindered, as plainly spread out before him as our dining table's bright red tablecloth. Here the anger was now, pulsating, coming off of me in waves. I pulled into our garage and turned off the ignition, grappling with his astounding betrayal. We both sat there in silence, in the dark, as though strengthening our nerves for a great battle.

"You're angry with me," Roy said.

"Yes."

"You're taking this too personally."

"I'm living with a man I don't know." I hated my querulous tone, but there it was. "You've become an unpredictable stranger."

"Let's not make this all about you, Anna."

"Is that what I do?" I began to cry. His tone was deeply injurious. "Make things all about me?"

Roy took a deep breath and smoothed his dwindling palms on the thighs of his pants. Watching him through my tears, I realized that he had shrunk another inch or two since the specialist's appointment. He was the size of a small child now. At this rate he would soon be gone forever.

"I'm sorry," I said, sitting up straighter and drying my eyes. It was my role as wife to take things upon myself, to ease his burdens. I swallowed my pride. "You're right, Roy, of course. It's not all about me. Come inside. I'll make you dinner. We must," I said bravely, "make the best of things."

I gathered my purse and keys and stepped out of the car. I turned to him and beckoned. A grateful expression of release – such a familiar expression to me – lightened his face. How easy it was, I mused, to sink back into the predictable rhythm of our marriage. It had always been this way: I set the sails, gathered the wind and controlled the rudder. I would guide us, as ever, to shore. He was my passenger, dutiful and thankful. As I opened the door to the kitchen, I heard his car door pock shut. He followed me into the house like a gentle puppy.

Nonetheless, as I tied my faded, patched apron around my waist – an apron that had been given to me as a wedding present, all those long decades ago – I drew a breath into my lungs and tasted the terrible vapor of Roy's screams. I shuddered involuntarily over the hot stove. A fearful thought came to me that perhaps Roy imagined leaving me.

I had never before been afraid of losing him. Rather, the opposite had always seemed more likely. *Oh how easily I could leave him*, I had always assumed, although my generosity of spirit forbade me to do so. Now, however, hearing him shake out the newspaper in the next room, his departure seemed not only possible, but imminent. I was sweating now, droplets of moisture rolling from my nose into the frying pan. I left them there with a feeling of revenge. If I had to breathe in his screams, then he would have to drink my sweat. A fair trade.

What a horrible night it was, the worst night in our entire marriage. The day's disturbing revelations had wrecked my appetite. While I poked weakly at my food, Roy sat across the table from me, eating ravenously. When he looked up and met my bewildered stare, I saw him not as my tall, gentle husband-of-many-years but as a short, cantankerous stranger, a stranger who had infiltrated my household with the sole desire to tear it apart. A shrinking man should be terribly insecure, but Roy was the opposite. The smaller his body became, the larger his confidence grew, as though he were changing from a man into an animal. Later, as we lay in bed, each of us pretending to be engrossed in whatever book we were reading that day, I wondered what he was thinking for the first time in years. *Penny for your thoughts*, I considered saying, but the adage was too trite. Was he thinking of me? Of leaving me? Was he thinking of how he had wasted his entire life?

I didn't ask.

Instead, I fell asleep and dreamed about ants. They were writhing over the poor carcass of a dead thing. I brushed them off over and over again, but they seemed only to multiply. An eyeball stared up at me from under the black squirming mass, blinking, wide with terror at its demise.

I awoke the next day with the taste of vomit in my mouth. I rushed down the stairs, calling for Roy. He was there, standing before the sink, trying to rinse out his cereal bowl, too short now to reach the tap. I took the bowl from him, grateful for my usefulness, and completed the task for him without a word. As the warm water poured through my fingers, I felt my fears melt away. Down, down the drain they vanished, along with the bowl's milk and grains. Here Roy was, still with me. Right here, at my elbow. He needed me now more than ever.

In the end, I needn't have worried so. All turned out quite well, considering.

Of course, Roy continued to shrink. We called the therapist and the second specialist, out of duty, really, but without hope. The therapist tried her hardest to reverse the process, this "growing backwards," as she called it, but it was in vain. She switched from working on his depression to working on his coping skills. "How to cope with extreme change" became a mantra in their meetings. Roy laughed about it with me at night, saying how silly it all was. His voice became high and squeaky, a little boy's voice, and I giggled with pleasure just to hear it.

The second specialist was more blunt: there was nothing to be done now, other than getting our papers in order. We should call our children and have them visit. We should prepare ourselves for the inevitability of his becoming no bigger than a speck of dust, of his disappearing entirely. What was unthinkable one day became old hat the next. Our children came to say goodbye. We rejoiced in their presence. We also rejoiced when they left, so exhausted were we by their emotional goodbyes and unyielding attentions. After the last car pulled away, we heaved a sigh of relief. The house was our own again.

Now that we had accepted Roy's fate, we began to have a sense of humor about it all. When we went out in public, people mistook him as my grandchild. *A child dressed as a little gentleman,* one poor woman said to us, putting her hand on Roy's shoulder, only to shriek in horror and shock when the wrinkled face of an old man glowered up at her in response. This sent us into giant guffaws of hilarity later, recalling with pleasure her frightened scream and fumbling apologies.

In the evenings, when he had become as small as a cat, he would curl up on my lap and I would read poetry to him, stroking his head. He began to understand less and less, his brain diminishing in size and ability, but I cherished our closeness nonetheless.

Finally, no bigger than my forefinger, he became constantly startled by my presence, as if I were a great cloud passing through the sky and blocking out the sun. I learned to move slowly around him, to avoid sending him into a panic. More than ever he needed me, and I lavished my full attention on him as gently and generously as possible.

The therapist ended their appointments at about this time, citing Roy's loss of cognizance. She insisted that I visit her instead. For an hour a week, I sat in her office with Roy in a shoebox on my lap, mourning his transformation. I cried and moaned, allowed the tears to run down my cheeks unhindered. I clawed at her couch cushion's golden tassels. "Why me?" I pleaded. The therapist nodded and listened with a sad, pleased expression. I was experiencing all of the stages of grief in ideal succession. I was the perfect patient, much as I had been the perfect wife.

It was after one such emotive session when, back home, exhausted from my performance, I lifted off the cover of the shoebox and found in it – instead of my tiny husband – a delicate brown cricket. It was what he had been changing into all along. He had finally become what I had always wanted him to be: a fragile being, a thing to be protected and cherished. A thing to be loved. Looking down into his empty insect's eyes, I began to weep. I was overwhelmed with tenderness. *Oh,* I said to him, wishing I could kiss his infinitesimal mouth, *oh my dear, dear husband. What a beautiful gift you've given me!*

My children returned, of course, for what they called a funeral. I did not argue with them, but welcomed them heartily. We walked to the alfalfa fields not far from our home. We deposited the open shoebox in a soft rut of sweet-smelling earth. The cricket inside leaped out of the box and, hitting the warm soil, went very still. My eldest daughter said a few loving words. The rest of them dissolved into various postures of emotional distress, and I comforted them the best I could. Finally, its courage restored, the cricket pounced away, into the corn stalks, leaving us all behind. We returned home with our arms wrapped around one another. My children, I could tell, were cleansed.

They adored their father. They couldn't relinquish his old self to this new one. They couldn't understand why I insisted on taking care of the cricket, on loving it with the same devotion that I had always accorded Roy.

And that's why I went to the pet store, why I purchased one cricket, just one, from the giant tank teeming with them, why I placed this impostor cricket in a shoebox and presented it to my children as their father.

The real Roy, thankfully, remains with me.

At night I take out the shoebox and hold Roy in the palm of my hand. He flutters the remainder of his wings. I had to clip them, you see, to stop the constant chirping. It is a pleasant sound at first, but after a week it grows quite irksome. He didn't feel a thing, I promise you. He didn't even wince. Just look at his tiny infinite face. At the bottom of those expressionless eyes, there is a deep contentment.

Thank you, my wife, those eyes say. *Thank you for all that you've done for me.*

FIELD GUIDE TO MONSTERS
OF THE INLAND NORTHWEST

The Projectionist waved to his wife. She stood in the back corner of the conference room, hidden mostly in shadow. With her normal bashful slowness – a slowness he understood as part of her good-hearted nature – she responded with a thumbs-up sign. Even in shadow, even from across the vast room, he could see that her thumbs were twice as large as his own thumbs, and his heart gave a faint little leap. He had a sudden desire to tell her to flee, as if worried that the growing crowd would soon fall upon her with torches and pitchforks.

The speaker approached him and touched his arm. Dr. Roebuck. He had once been a famous podiatrist – as famous as a podiatrist can be, that is – but had left his practice to study giant humanlike footprints found in the Selkirk Mountains, not far from where he lived in Post Falls, Idaho. He had first studied these prints as a skeptic, or so he declared at the many conferences where he spoke, but after months of analysis and fieldwork, he became convinced that the tracks were, in fact, the footprints of a humanoid. He eventually found other tracks in the mountains, not only in the Selkirks but also in the Cabinets and in the Coeur d'Alenes, and he even located one impressively sized pair heading straight into Lake Pend Oreille. This impelled him to write a controversial essay called *Sasquatch: The Lake's Strongest Swimmer*, published in *Cryptozoology Monthly*. His latest field work, completed recently in the Bitterroots, was purported to hold his most exciting findings yet, and he was unfurling these findings tonight at the conference, having hired the Projectionist to run the slide show from his computer as he always did. The only thing strange was that Dr. Roebuck had explicitly requested that the Projectionist bring his wife.

The Projectionist was an admirer of Dr. Roebuck's, but not exactly for his work with the cryptids, which he privately found spotty, over-dramatized at best. He admired how polite Dr. Roebuck was, how well-spoken. He admired the way he dressed, which was inscrutably neat: patterned sweater vests with smooth ironed pants, tailored dress shirts and clever cufflinks. On Dr. Roebuck's narrow nose perched a pair of bright red tortoise-shell glasses, sharpening his blue eyes into two round bits of steel.

The Projectionist, preferring to work and live in the background, did not pay close attention to how he himself dressed, so that sometimes when he emerged from his closet his wife would put her hairy hand up to her mouth and giggle affectionately. The Projectionist couldn't help but smile back at her and smirk at himself in the mirror, wearing perhaps, as he was tonight, glittering spandex pants with cowboy boots, a bola tie over a ribbed tank top, a bright green golf visor mashed onto his forehead. His wife was an impeccable dresser – she sewed all of her own clothes so that they fit her perfectly. Tonight she wore a simple paisley dress that hit her knees lightly when she walked. On her head was a cream-colored pillbox hat, complete with a fashionable veil. It was not the sort of thing women wore in the twenty-first century, but she pulled off such anachronistic styles with aplomb. Like many large women with good taste, The Projectionist's wife understood how to offset her size with delicate accoutrements. The veil, he thought, was the perfect touch, softening as it did the tremendous bushiness of her brow.

Such good taste, the Projectionist now mused, allowing Dr. Roebuck to guide him away from the podium, *Such good taste and she chose me!* He marveled at his luck. Since his meeting her, his life had gone from pathetic to enviable. Such generosity of spirit, such candor and grace, he had never before encountered in a person. His friends thought he was crazy, his parents almost disowned him, but now they saw how fruitful the marriage was, how beneficial to all parties involved, and they either grew to love his wife or at least learned to keep their opinions and jokes to themselves. His mom now even pushed for them to have children, and he had noted with satisfaction the soft glimmer of hope in his wife's eyes at the last overt urging.

Dr. Roebuck stopped him beside the laptop, giving the Projectionist's elbow a friendly squeeze before releasing him. He was looking somewhat hungrily around the room. "I trust you brought your wife?"

"Yes, of course, she's come with me." The Projectionist gestured toward the hulking figure that lurked beside the rows of light panels. "I've put her in charge of the dimmers."

Dr. Roebuck's face erupted into a smile of relief. "Ah, marvelous," he murmured. "She's a perfect specimen."

The Projectionist, nonplussed, asked the doctor what he meant.

"I only mean to say that she's marvelous," he said hurriedly, glancing at the Projectionist with a sheepish look. "I've heard that she's a marvelous woman."

22

"She *is*," the Projectionist replied. He felt a bit defensive, although he wasn't sure why. After all, hadn't his wife just been complimented? He should say 'thank you.' But he couldn't help but wonder what Dr. Roebuck's motives were. He asked again why he was so adamant about his wife's attendance, but the doctor waved the question away with one hand.

"I merely wanted to meet this marvelous woman I've heard such marvelous things about," he said casually. Then, with a look of worry, "I hope I haven't offended you. I don't mean to undermine your work here."

The Projectionist suddenly felt foolish. "No, of course not," he rushed to say, and Dr. Roebuck's brow relaxed again. Geesh, the Projectionist chided himself. Wasn't it typical for bosses to request the presence of a loyal employee's wife? And wasn't Dr. Roebuck more than a boss after all of these years, after all of these conferences – wasn't he in fact more akin to a friend? And hadn't his wife told him that his biggest fault was distrusting people? Hadn't she teased him about not seeing goodness in any one other than herself? Oh, how well she knew him. How much he still had to learn!

"No, of course not," the Projectionist repeated. "She'll be delighted to meet you – "

"And if it's a matter of money," Dr. Roebuck said abruptly, turning back to him, "rest assured, there is money in it for you. I've already written out an impressive bonus, to be delivered to you tomorrow, if all goes well."

The Projectionist paled. "If what goes well, Doctor?"

Dr. Roebuck smiled at the Projectionist kindly. "My presentation, of course."

There was a moment's silence.

Then the doctor asked, "What did you say your wife's name was, please?"

"Esmeralda," the Projectionist stammered. He then hurried on to ask, stopping himself from seizing the doctor's prim lapel, "But what, exactly, are you planning?"

The crowd surged then, the lights were dimmed (dutifully by his wife, who had been instructed to dim the lights at precisely five to the hour), and Dr. Roebuck parted from the panicked Projectionist with a simple instruction to relax. The Projectionist glanced over his shoulder for his wife. He could not see her – she had backed further into the shadows now that the crowd had increased, as though afraid that she might recognize someone. Her absence frightened him. Of course, he told himself, he was being silly. She was not in any mortal danger. Why was he so nervous?

He leaned over his computer and loaded the presentation. Then he straightened and awaited Dr. Roebuck's signal, a slight touching of the eyebrow that would command the Projectionist to hit "play." Predictably, as the hour struck, Dr. Roebuck rose from his modest chair at the front of the room, turning toward the crowd and congenially touching his right eyebrow as though bidding them good day. Grateful to toss himself back into his work, the Projectionist pushed his finger against the space bar, and the giant white screen behind the podium became illuminated with the brilliant cover of Dr. Roebuck's soon-to-be-published opus, *Field Guide to Monsters of the Inland Northwest*. Dr. Roebuck looked up at the screen in admiration. He let the cover image sink into the crowd – a large, hairy humanoid carrying a beautiful weeping woman over his shoulder. The humanoid was slouching through dense forest, and in the background you could see what was presumably his cave, the ground littered with human skulls. The crowd gave an admiring gasp and then applauded lightly. Dr. Roebuck fiddled with the headset he always wore for his presentations, adjusting it so that the microphone hovered just before his thin lips. Then he teased the crowd by saying, as though he were stupid, "Is this gosh-darn thing even on?" to which they laughed and called out, "Oh, yes!" and "We can hear you perfectly, Doctor!" The Projectionist always found these affectations cornballish, but the crowd always fell for it, and the Projectionist supposed that his annoyance with such behavior was why he was in the background and the doctor in the foreground. Calmer now in the darkness, the Projectionist took a moment to look for his wife, and saw her standing not too far from him, staring at the screen with a look of awe on her face. The Projectionist felt such relief upon seeing her that the doctor's recent interest in her fell from his mind. The doctor wrapped up the discussion of the cover art. The Projectionist, properly prepped about when to proceed, pushed the button for the next slide.

For the next hour, Dr. Roebuck discussed the contents of his new book. Mostly they were based on the humanoids, e.g. Bigfoot. Dr. Roebuck believed that each mountainous region had its own species, some of them smaller than others, some of them with reddish fur, others with black fur, most of them with brownish fur. But his book also explored other legends: the great monster who lurked in the depths of Lake Pend Oreille, the "Pend Oreille Paddler", which, Dr. Roebuck assured everyone, he had proof was in fact a monster and not, as the navy said, a submarine that was being tested for acoustics in the deep waters, although the lake certainly had those, too; a man-sized tick sucking the blood from moose and elk in the Coeur

d'Alenes; and finally the Northwest Centaurs, half-man, half-elk beasts –
not extinct as had been the rumors, but thriving in the dry inland forests,
sometimes maltreated as pests (and poisoned illegally, to the chagrin of Dr.
Roebuck) in community gardens where they nibbled on the buds of native
flowers. Each slide featured beautiful illustrations of the creatures, as well
as some photographs of Dr. Roebuck in the field, and the Projectionist
looked around the large conference room and saw these images glowing
softly in the wide eyeballs of the enrapt crowd. He saw in their raised chins
and drunken expressions that they were, all of them, transported – even
his wife – by the idea of things magical among them. It was, the Projectionist thought, the best conference yet.

He hit the last slide, which was filled with quotations (several blurbs
for Dr. Roebuck's new book) and his wife, recognizing the image, slowly
turned up the lights in the conference room, again as per her instructions.
The Projectionist left his laptop running so that the advanced praise on
the screen hung over Dr. Roebuck as he took questions from the audience.
The Projectionist tuned this portion out, beginning to gather some of his
items together so as to make for a quicker departure when the doctor
finished (he hated these crowds, and his stomach was rumbling slightly,
indicating the beginnings of a gnawing hunger). The questions droned
on around him, but he didn't care to listen – they were normally the same
questions conference to conference, and there was always a skeptic or two
and always someone who loved the sound of his or her own voice, asking
something worthless but long-winded. Having gathered his coat and brief-
case and most of the computer wires, letting it run now on its battery, the
Projectionist turned to find his wife, and saw her large frame pressing into
the wall, her eyes wide and her mouth slightly ajar, listening with much
interest. He could not catch her gaze now. She was under Dr. Roebuck's
spell, her imagination teeming.

"Now," Dr. Roebuck said suddenly, putting up a hand to signal an
end to the question-and-answer period. "Now I'd like to do something special. We have a creature here today that I am sure is a descendant of the
humanoids, specifically of the Bitterroot region. I'd like to ask her to come
up here, if she wouldn't mind, and I've heard she's quite shy – also a characteristic of the species, I might add – so if everyone would please put their
hands together and give her a warm welcome, I'm sure we can cajole her
to join us."

The crowd applauded. Voices murmured in anticipation. The Projectionist automatically brought his hands together, but something wobbled

in his heart as he clapped, and a dark feeling sprouted like wings from his shoulder blades and flapped coldly around him. He knew what name the doctor would call. Pitchforks and torches.

"Esmeralda," Dr. Roebuck said loudly. "The wife of my projectionist. He's so talented, folks, putting together these slideshows. Let's give him some applause, as well."

This was the first time that the doctor had acknowledged his efforts publicly. The Projectionist blushed. The crowd's attention slammed into him like a large warm wave. He swam through it, disoriented. Desperately, as though for help, he turned to Esme. There she was, watching him, her face a waxen contortion of surprise. The Projectionist shrugged, *I didn't know*, he tried to mouth, but her look of surprise melted into confusion as she tried to interpret his lips. The crowd was applauding louder now, following the Projectionist's gaze and seeing, for the first time, the "creature" that Dr. Roebuck spoke of with such certainty, seeing that she was, indeed, hulking and hairy. Someone from the back row jumped up and took her arm. He guided her to the front of the room as though escorting her onto a dance floor. He was a small man, overdressed in a tuxedo, and she towered over him, making him look no bigger than a child. It was her gentle nature, the Projectionist knew, that allowed her to be so easily led. He could see in her face when she pivoted back toward the room that she was terrified. Dr. Roebuck reached out and touched her arm in a delicate manner that made the Projectionist almost grateful. *Be kind to her,* he wanted to cry out. But would that cause his wife more embarrassment? The crowd gazed at her rapturously, their thousand eyes shining.

"Note the large brow," Dr. Roebuck said, holding a yardstick up to Esmeralda's face, causing her to blink. "Note the heavy hairline that stretches from one ear, over her brow, all the way to the other ear. This, especially, denotes the species – the other humanoids have beards, male or female, but the Bitterroot species does not. Now, for her hands," he gingerly touched Esmeralda's wrist, indicating that she raise it, which she did. "Note the thumbs – double jointed, as is typical – and how long they are, nearly twice the size of an average man's thumb." Again, with the yardstick. "Do you see the slight webbing between the fingers? This shows that, like the Pend Oreille species, the Bitterroot humanoids were once excellent swimmers."

He lowered Esmeralda's hand and went silent for a moment, considering her. The Projectionist watched anxiously, hoping that this indicated the finale of the spectacle. If it ended now, he thought, the damage would be minimal. He and his wife might even laugh over this on the way home, and any injured feelings could quickly be kissed away. The Projectionist saw her eyes pinned on him, the whites of her eyeballs enormous like those on a frightened horse, but she managed to give him a faint, brave smile – her affections were still intact.

But then, after a moment, Dr. Roebuck turned back to the crowd, shaking his head. "You see," he said sadly. "I want to ask this gentle beast –"

Woman, the Projectionist inwardly lamented, *She's a woman for crissakes.*

" – to do something quite unconventional. It is, of course, the nature of the Bitterroot species to be eager-to-please, so if I only ask her, she will comply. But we must ask her husband if this is alright, so as to not offend any of my colleagues."

Dr. Roebuck clasped his hands together in a demure gesture of entreaty. Eyes pivoted in the direction the hands indicated, landing with one giant swoop – like heavy birds landing on a wire – on the Projectionist. Dr. Roebuck waited patiently, his hands still clasped. This gesture startled the Projectionist – the doctor, inadvertently or no, was placing the treatment of his wife in his own hands. A moment ago, the Projectionist was ready to fight. Now his knees shook. With all of these other eyes upon him, the Projectionist could not meet Esmeralda's tender, pleading face. He dropped his gaze to his feet and stood there, undecided, for several moments. Hadn't the doctor treated her kindly so far, considering? Hadn't he touched her wrist gently? They must be nearing the end of this examination, surely? He gauged that there would only be another five minutes of torture at the most. Then he and his wife could go home. He thought about the generous bonus the doctor had promised. He would take his wife out for a fancy meal to apologize. Maybe buy her something beautiful, a necklace or a gold watch, something he normally could not afford.

Slowly, slowly, without lifting his gaze, the Projectionist nodded his head. With relief, he felt the heavy sets of eyes lift away from him and fly back to the front of the room. His once-white sneakers had become in the recent wet weeks turd brown, covered with mud and filth. Off to the left of one of his shoes, a small spider hurried past, probably en route to his own home in some comfortable dusty corner somewhere. Someone behind him saw the spider and stamped on it, and then the spider became a squiggle of guts on the carpet. This filled the Projectionist with more dread than he'd ever thought imaginable, and his head snapped up, and he met his wife's blank gaze. She had her eyes locked on him as the doctor asked

27

her – kindly, always so kindly – to remove her dress, *What a lovely gown,* and to please, also, remove her bra and to, if she wouldn't mind, please remove her underwear, oh, and also her knee-high socks, *charming, aren't they? Humanoids are excellent craftsmen, as you can see by her hand-sewn garments.* The Projectionist's wife then stood there, before the crowd, stark naked. Voices rose excitedly around them, sounds of appreciation, sounds of amusement, sounds of fear. It occurred to him suddenly that some of these sounds – the small, almost inaudible whimpering, for example – were coming from his own mouth.

The yardstick did more measuring, the doctor droned on, and all in all his wife stood before the crowd, stoically, for another thirty minutes. The whole while, she stared at her husband, and he stared back at her, and at one point – his eyesight beginning to blur from the heat in the crowd and also from the infrequency of his blinking – he saw her as the crowd saw her: enormous, hirsute, terrifying; a creature, with some similarities to a woman, but mostly another thing unto itself. An *It*, he thought. For a moment, this thought was comforting to him. An *It*, of course, had no feelings. An *It* would not be angry with him for standing by so helplessly. An *It* would go home, hold his hand in the car, smile when he wanted *It* to smile, cook him a rich stew, slip into bed with him unharmed. But the relief was momentary, as was his dehumanization of her. For the very next moment, she grimaced when the doctor spread her legs apart, and the Projectionist saw her not as an *It* at all, but as his loving, gentle wife, who was now having all of her privates shown to a large crowd.

Do something, he screamed to himself. With robot's legs, he strode toward the front of the room. Dr. Roebuck, seeing his approach, raised his eyebrows in alarm and then wrapped up his speech abruptly, "Well, I think that's all we have time for today. Go ahead and get dressed, Esmeralda. Let's give her a round of applause, everyone," and the crowd jumped to their feet so that the Projectionist had to battle his way through their teeming bodies. It smelled like sweat in the conference room, ripe and malodorous, and the Projectionist worried for a moment that he might vomit. Some of the people assembled began to leave, pushing him backwards, and still others decided to meet and perhaps even touch the Projectionist's beastly wife, flowing toward the front of the room, shaking hands with the doctor and waiting patiently in line for introductions to the humanoid. *The humanoid,* everyone was saying, *Sasquatch's daughter. Not a bad looker,* a fat man in a hunting cap said to his equally portly companion. *Can't say*

I'd marry her, but she would be fuckable after a few beers. The Projectionist elbowed this man out of his way, and the man protested for a moment but then recognized him and said, *There's the husband. Looks like a real loony. Ignore him,* the Projectionist told himself, and he did so, pushing past the gathered bodies until he finally reached the one body that meant something to him: his wife's.

She had reassembled her clothes and pinned her hat back onto her head (her careful coiffure was now mussed), and she stood there smiling meekly at the people who pressed against her. At first glance, she looked undisturbed by the whole matter, but then the Projectionist noticed that her dress was on backwards. One of her ears was bleeding slightly from where she had stabbed it with a pin. He reached forward and grasped her hand, and she, startled, returned the grasp so resolutely that he nearly screamed. Then, seeing it was her husband, she relaxed somewhat, but her countenance remained unfamiliar to him: guarded, flustered, distrustful.

"I was trying to come forward," he hurriedly whispered to her, standing on his tiptoes so he could reach her ear. "I was fighting to get to the front of the room."

"What?" she said, and he realized that in the din of the crowd, she couldn't hear him.

"Oh my," a young woman said, coming forward and shaking Esmeralda's free hand. She was wearing a bra on the outside of her t-shirt. Her jeans had giant holes in the thighs. "Such a pleasure to meet you. Your husband must be so proud."

Esmeralda said nothing, but the Projectionist gushed, "Oh yes!"

"Tell me something," the young woman said, smiling back at the Projectionist, leaning forward confidentially. "Does she have any cousins or brothers or anything? You know? Male humanoids? I sure would be interested in meeting one of them. Strong and gentle and hardworking. Rough in bed, I'm sure. Just my type."

The Projectionist was surprised by the question. Truthfully, he didn't know. He looked up at Esmeralda, who was studying the young woman quietly. She had never wanted to speak of her family, and the Projectionist had always respected her silence. He figured that something extremely painful had happened to them, something that Esmeralda clearly wanted to forget. Besides, she always said that he was the only family she would ever need.

"Dead," she said now, with such ferocity that the young woman frowned and took a step backwards. The coldness in her voice was so very foreign that the Projectionist wondered if the word had been uttered by someone other than his wife, but then she repeated it. "All of them. Dead."

Dr. Roebuck, hearing her response, came forward and tapped on the mike. The remaining groups of people turned politely toward him.

"I believe our friendly humanoid is quite tired," he said. "It's been a long day for her and her husband. Let's leave them in peace, shall we? After all, the last thing we want is a tired, angry humanoid on our hands. They can become quite dangerous when cranky."

Esmeralda released the Projectionist's hand then, turning toward the fire exit at the back of the conference room. The crowds grumbled but respectfully fell away. Some of them snapped a last photograph with their cell phones or with cameras the size of cigarette boxes. The Projectionist jogged after his wife. She was moving away quickly and he could barely keep up.

"Esme," he called. "Esme."

She pushed through the backdoor, setting off an alarm, and then, with a loud sob, hurtled herself toward the truck. The Projectionist felt as though his heart would break. He had seen his wife cry before, but always out of happiness.

"Esme," he said again, as they settled into the truck. "I tried to reach you. I tried to get through the crowd, to save you."

She mashed her face in her hands, shaking her head. She uttered something, but the sound was muffled. Gently asking her to repeat what she had said, he reached over and massaged her broad neck.

"When?" She lifted her face from her hands. Her eyes were puffy, her cheeks mottled. "When did you try to reach me? You *let* them do this to me. You *gave* them permission. I saw you. I saw you look at me the way *they* looked at me. Do you think I'm a monster, too?"

The Projectionist shook his head, frowning. "Of course not." But then he remembered the night they had met. He had been spelunking with a college roommate, and had just emerged from the darkness to sit atop a grotto that overlooked the forest canopy. The dry pines swung in the breeze. Across the starlight, their tips swept like dark paintbrushes. His wife had emerged from a black grove of trees, dressed simply in a tank top and chinos, the night being warm, and she had taken a seat beside him, saying, "Isn't it a lovely night?"

He was taken aback by the size and confidence of this woman. Despite the primitive angles of her face, and despite the hairy brow, she had lovely skin and a sweet demeanor. He had asked if she had been spelunking, too, and she shuddered. "Oh no," she said, "I hate the caves. I've been walking around in the forest."

"At night?" he said, impressed.

"Oh yes. I always walk through the forest at night."

When he had asked where she lived, she had waved her hand in the direction of Newport, and he had naturally assumed she meant one of the small villages up north. Now, he thought, maybe she had meant the guts of the forest. Why hadn't he been more curious? And would it have made a difference either way? What did it even matter?

He continued to knead her neck as he drove. "I don't care if you're a monster or not," he said firmly. "I love you regardless."

She sobbed again – once, loudly – and then removed his hand from her neck.

Later that night, at home, the Projectionist sat on their dusty, sturdy sofa, watching his wife as she stood at the window. He was waiting for a sign that he had been forgiven. "I want things to be like they were this morning," he said plaintively. "Why does this morning feel so far away?"

Esmeralda smiled faintly. This comment seemed to amuse her. "It *is* far away," she said. "It's lost." She peered out the window again, her smile fading as though she awaited some terrible visitor. "They'll change their minds. People always start out as curious. Then the curiosity turns to fear. They'll come after us." She turned to look at her husband, and he saw for the first time in hours a flicker of her old love for him, tempered now, but not dead. "I've seen it happen before."

The Projectionist rose and went to stand beside her. Down where the road curved toward town, he saw a flame glow and waver. Torches, he thought. Pitchforks. He marveled at his clairvoyance. How had he known? How had he been able to predict this outcome?

The flame vanished.

"Bed," his wife said, and he obeyed. He fell asleep with surprising ease, grateful that she let him snuggle against her warm heft.

In the morning, she was gone. All of her beautifully sewn garments hung in the closet. Her leather shoes sat on the floor next to the furnace, as though she had decided to flee barefoot. The oven and coffee pot were cold – she had taken no food, no clothing, no money. The Projectionist sat at the cheerless kitchen table. He knew she wouldn't return.

A knock at the door. The Projectionist rose to answer it, his face numb, unsmiling. A courier in a red cap handed him an envelope: the large check from Dr. Roebuck, as promised. He had penned on the check's memo line, *For the use of your marvelous wife: thank you.*

The Projectionist put his head in his hands. He wept, chiding himself for his spinelessness.

If only I'd left her at home that day, If only I'd refused the doctor, If only I'd reached her earlier, If only I'd sucker-punched him, If only I'd apologized more convincingly, If only I'd woken up before she tiptoed out of my life forever.

The Projectionist wiped his eyes and stared at the check. It was ample, and would easily cover his mortgage for the next year. He considered walking to the bank directly to make a deposit. Then, with hardly a moment's thought, he took the check between his forefinger and thumb and tore it apart. It burned a moment later in the fireplace, hardly long enough for the Projectionist to enjoy it, but he enjoyed it nonetheless. In the few short moments in which it ignited and blazed, he wondered, as he often would, if his wife were watching from the woods.

If only I'd never met her.

No, that was wrong.

If only she'd never met me.

For he was sure that he had caused her more heartbreak and misery than she had ever caused him.

VVVVVVVVVVVVVVVVVVVVVVVVV

SOUVENIRS

∧∧∧∧∧∧∧∧∧∧∧∧∧∧∧∧∧∧∧∧∧∧∧∧∧

He was my serial killer. I call him mine because he lived across the street from me. Some people would find this worrisome, frightening even. Not me. I grew up in Spokane. There are rapists and serial killers and pedophiles on most street corners in Spokane, and it gets to the point that if you're walking through Riverfront Park and the rapist/serial killer/pedophile happens to be approaching from the other direction, you may as well just smile and greet him like you would anyone else. This doesn't happen on the West Side. I know, because my ex is from Seattle, and he never said hello to anyone.

The market for serial killer belongings is really booming in the Northwest. I met a man once who had a mountain bike and a power drill, each from one of the most notorious serial killers produced by Washington State. I was jealous of such a hobby. Not that I couldn't collect them, too. You can purchase almost anything off of eBay. But for me, it's hard to be passionate about something that someone else has already coveted.

My serial killer kept a neat and trim lawn. We lived in a typical Spokane neighborhood, where people liked their yards more than their neighbors and spent thousands of dollars each year on prolific watering systems. His lawn was arguably the best lawn on our block. Much nicer than my lawn, which I weeded only once, in the spring, when I briefly dedicated myself to the healthful growing of things. Then my dedication waned and armies of dandelions took over and choked out the brown grass. In comparison my serial killer's lawn was like the Elysian Fields, with marigolds and cosmos edging the smooth grass trim, shaded here and there by carefully manicured fruit trees. A fake owl perched nobly on the edge of the fence, keeping a steady vigil on my rented house. Up close the owl was cross-eyed, giving her a nerdy and harmless sort of appeal, but from across the street she was an impressive predator.

My serial killer's name was Rold. A weird name. A Viking name. Sometimes he would fold his lanky arms over his chest and study his yard for long minutes at a time. Then he would shake his head over something unsatisfactory that I couldn't see, saying as he did so, "Tut tut." This was not the sort of thing you would expect a Viking serial killer to say, "Tut tut." But that's what he said. Always, disapprovingly, "Tut tut," as though it cleared his mind somehow.

It was one of the first details I learned about him, in fact, a few weeks before I discovered that he was a serial killer. We had just moved in, my ex and I. I had been watching Rold, rather obviously, from the cracked wicker hanging-chair of my porch. I liked to watch how industrious he was in his little yard. Even then there was something special in the way he worked. Even then I could sense he had dark secrets. I found him oddly attractive. I was thinking about this attractiveness and swinging slowly in the hanging-chair when he suddenly looked up and saw me watching him. He beckoned for me to cross the street. I did.

In his yard, I toed a hill of pea gravel that he was spreading with a rake onto his walkway. I was wearing a pair of white sneakers that came away speckled with tan dust.

"You have a lovely yard," I said.

Rold frowned over his rake and then straightened. He surveyed his garden and his little pathway and he sighed. It was early spring, and a small stubborn pile of snow still lingered in the shade near his trellis. He shook his head and said, "Tut tut." I giggled in response, delighted with the phrase's archaic charm. He didn't seem to notice my amusement.

"Ah," he said. "There's so much work to do." Then he leaned over his rake and began spreading the pea gravel again. He glanced up at me and winked. "But just wait. Come summer, it will be a masterpiece."

I nodded, noticing how strong and long and pale his hands were. They were artisans' hands, capable of anything. The rake against the gravel made a hissing, rasping sound, a sound that anyone else would have found grating, but I found it satisfying, vivifying; the sound of good work being done. I asked him if he wanted some help.

"Thank you, no," he said. He looked at me with his merry eyes. "I just noticed you watching me. I thought you might want a closer look. What's your name?"

"Sarah," I said. "What's yours?"

He told me his name. Then he said, "How old are you?"

"I just turned thirty-one." I raised my chin a little to show him I wasn't lying. I looked young for my age – not in a good way – and I expected him to say something about it.

"Happy birthday," he said. He continued raking. "I don't mean to be presumptuous, of course. You *were* watching me, weren't you?"

"Well, yes," I said. "I'm very observant."

He laughed at this. If he laughed nervously, I didn't notice. After all, how could he know then that I already liked him, despite what I would eventually learn?

"I'm glad you've moved here then," he said. "We need observant neighbors."

I shrugged. "I'm just nosy, that's all."

The rake slid back and forth. The gray hill of gravel steadily flattened. "There is a lot of darkness in the world," he said. "Vigilance is a virtue."

It was then that we heard a muffled scream. We both straightened and stared at one another for a moment.

"What was that?" I said.

The sound had come from the direction of his house. We waited for a few moments, tensed. But then all was still. The white clapboards of his house were freshly painted and clean in the dim sun. His front door was painted a dark brownish red.

Rold shrugged and returned to raking. "I don't know," he said. Then, absently, "I left the television on."

He was raking forcefully now, and even if there had been another scream I would perhaps not have heard it. I wasn't worried about it, anyway. It could have been a child next door, or a crow, I reasoned, or an animal that had hurt itself behind his house. A squirrel with a twisted ankle.

My ex's car rounded the corner. I extended a mitten-enclosed hand to Rold. I was fully decked out for winter, and it suddenly occurred to me that Rold was underdressed for the season – no gloves, no coat. I was impressed. "It's a pleasure meeting you, Rold," I said. "I better get going now."

Rold stopped raking and leaned the rake against his shoulder. He accepted my hand in both hands, shaking gently. "The pleasure is all mine," he said. My ex slammed his car door and stood in front of our house, holding a large cardboard box with the words XBOX STUFF written in black Sharpie across its side. He waited for me without a smile. Rold's eyes trailed to him and he smirked.

"Is that your husband?"

"Boyfriend," I said.

"Is he also vigilant?"

I shook my head, "Not so much, no."

Rold grinned. "Don't be a stranger now, Sarah." He leaned back over his rake. "We recluses must stick together."

I wasn't sure how he guessed I was a recluse, but I wasn't offended. If anything, I was happy to find someone as accepting of his own alienation as I was mine.

•

This was the same year I worked at the espresso drive-through. I had been laid off from my previous job as a filing clerk, a job that had been easy and that I had liked for the repetition and solitude. I was desperate for cash. The drive-through was the first job I could find. The boss had hired me despite the fact – or perhaps because of the fact – that I had become tongue-tied and teary-eyed when he mentioned that I might be a little old for the job.

My co-worker, Sam, was twenty. She looked great in her headset. The round black bulb of the microphone floated like a forbidden fruit before her glossy nude lips. My headset, in comparison, conjured images of head-braces and medieval torture devices. It was our different facial features that created such a contrast. Sam had big sensual lips and oval eyes, and she always appeared sedated, post-orgasmic, no matter how many triple grande mochas she'd quaffed in the last half hour. I was thin-lipped, with the sprouting ears and bulging eyes of a tarsier.

Customers loved her. Men in the drive-through lingered for a few moments after she handed them their lattes and change. They blinked up at her wistfully while she took another car's order, her hand lightly touching the headset near her ear and causing one of the exotic pendulums of her earrings to swing. With me, the customers made little eye contact. They accelerated quickly out of the drive-through, onto bigger and better things, maybe wives waiting for them at home, or friendly upbeat girlfriends, or both. "It's the lack of make-up, Sarah," my ex once told me. "Can't you get some free makeover downtown? At Nordstrom? Riverpark Square?"

I could, and I tried, but afterwards I looked at myself in the mirror and saw some crazy neon clown staring back at me, and I had gone straight home and frantically scrubbed every ounce of it away. Later, relieved to be myself again, I told my ex that I hoped he still thought of me as beautiful, make-up or no. "You're fine," he said. "We're all uglier than someone, you know?" He gave my shoulder a squeeze and went back to watching Monster Trucks on television. There was some real truth to what he said, and I hugged him back and leaned against him on the couch, feeling sincerely that it was good to accept one's place in the world. Nonetheless, I shuddered with pity a few moments later when the larger monster truck rolled back and forth over a defenseless sedan, crushing it to smithereens.

My ex found Sam attractive. I knew this because he asked her out a few moments before he asked me out. She was handing over his double shot espresso in a 16 oz cup, no cream, no sugar (a sexy drink, I thought at the time), when he offered from his car seat to buy her dinner. She laughed and said no. I was behind Sam, wiping down the steamer. "How about you?" he said, calling to me through the coffee window. "Pasta tonight?" I said yes so loudly that Sam winced. She said later that it had made me seem desperate. But that night he pulled the chair out for me and offered me a cigarette after dessert. I don't smoke, but still I thought it was a classy move.

Regardless, it was clear from the beginning that we wouldn't end well. I wasn't his type. Sam was his type, or any other pretty girl that wore stylish clothes and blue eye shadow and perfume in her hair. I had scentless deodorant, sensitive skin. I tried to use good-smelling shampoos and soaps but to no avail. "You have an uncanny ability to neutralize smells," my ex once said. His tone suggested that this trait was creepy, like I was some strange scentless alien roaming wild on Planet Earth. Even in the beginning, even when things were great, his tone and behaviors suggested that he didn't quite approve of me. If we met some other girl that he knew, someone he worked with every day at his medical technician job, some pretty girl named Sally that shared a cubicle with him but that I had never heard about until this exact moment of meeting her on the street, he would forget to introduce me. I would stand there, long-armed and awkward, and the girl would smile at him and then glance at me expectantly and then smile at him again, clearly uncomfortable. Despite her obvious curiosity, he didn't mention me unless the girl intervened. I was like a dog he was taking for a walk.

But when we were alone he was always polite. He always held open my coat so I could slip my arms effortlessly into the sleeves. He always pulled out a chair for me and offered up the last French fry. He always let me choose where to go out for dinner. It probably didn't matter to him, since he disapproved of most places in Spokane.

Before he moved back to Seattle, he told me I could follow him, but he also told me that he couldn't promise he'd be my boyfriend there. I considered the move seriously for a few moments, but then I shook my head, no. I was made for Spokane, and we both knew it. There was no way I could leave. I was over thirty now and had never escaped, and now it was in my blood, heavy like liquid cement. I could feel myself walking slower and slower until he drove away, and then I stood on the corner of our little street feeling the cement gather heavily into my feet, and I watched his car zip down Southeast Boulevard, away from our house, off toward I-90. His radio blared as he drove away. He was free.

·

The night before my ex moved away, I went on a major crying jag. After I calmed down, my ex gave me one of the muscle relaxants his doctor prescribed for his TMJ. He told me it would help me sleep.

Despite the drug, I woke up sweating in the sheets a few hours later. It was near midnight. I rose groggily and went to the window. I put my palms on the pane and the cold shocked me awake. Outside, across the dark street, Rold wrestled with an object heavy and black. The moon had set. I could faintly make out the new raised bed he'd constructed only the day before, as well as a spade and a dark pile of soil. He hoisted his purchase into the deep empty bed. I saw, then, that the thing was bucking and kicking against him halfheartedly, like a thing drugged. Whatever it was appeared to be wrapped, mummylike, in layers of landscape fabric.

I said my ex's name – lowly, urgently. He moaned in his sleep.

"You need to see this," I hissed.

"Christ." He rolled over, dragging his pillow with him. "Sarah, I was dreaming about zombies." He said this as if he wanted the dream to go on forever.

"Something's going on," I said. "I can't tell for sure but it looks like Rold's burying someone alive."

My ex half-laughed, half-moaned. "Wouldn't surprise me. Crazy Spokanites." He pulled the pillow over his head and turned over.

I didn't reply. I watched Rold scooping earth into the narrow black hole. He did not seem hurried or nervous. A car drove by and its headlights momentarily alighted Rold's toiling silhouette. He did not even flinch.

"He's almost finished," I said. "You really should see this."

My ex flopped over, grimacing. "I don't need to see it. I don't give a shit. But if you're that concerned about it, then maybe we should call the cops. Hell, I'll call them, so long as you promise to come to bed."

This is what I had been considering, calling the cops, but when my ex suggested it I suddenly loathed the idea. Something in my heart wouldn't allow Rold to be ratted out. Especially not by my ex, who took such pleasure in pointing out negatives. I thought of my various conversations with Rold. He was the only neighbor who spoke to me, the only neighbor who spoke to anyone. The careful way he tended to his garden, the way his long

38

fingers gingerly arranged those fragile roots into the crumbling earth – perhaps whatever bad he did to others was cancelled out by his toil for good. Who were we to judge, anyway? My ex was destroying me daily, and I had become cruel to him, too, bitter that he didn't love me enough. Perhaps we were the ones who should be condemned.

I didn't say all of this to my ex. I only said, "Never mind. You're moving out. It's not your problem now." I moved toward the bed.

My ex sighed with relief. "Okay, then," he said in his teasing voice, "but when he chops off your head don't expect me to sing at your funeral."

My ex had always said he was an amazing singer, but he would never sing to me, despite my assurances that I would love it.

"Don't worry," I said. "I don't want a funeral, anyway. Just let me rot wherever I fall." I did not say this in self-pity. I was just being realistic.

In bed, my ex stroked my shoulder for a few minutes, the last time he would touch me before he left. Then his hand dropped away. He began to snore. I pictured his dreamland filled with friendly zombies, and I watched his calm, motionless face a little jealously before dropping into sleep, myself.

.

My serial killer was not as classically handsome as my ex, but he was far from unattractive. His eyebrows were so blonde as to seem transparent. He was almost fully bald except for a strip of light blonde hair that wrapped from ear to ear. He smiled a lot and his lanky shoulders were usually drooping forward like he was sleeping standing up. I am one of those people that always looks wired, like I've had five cups of coffee. I don't blink much. Even my hair stands up, because of the dryness inland, which creates extra static. My ex always suggested conditioner, and I would scream, "I'm wearing, like, five pounds of conditioner already!" And then he'd wax dreamily about the girls of Puget Sound and their soft moist hair.

Rold, though, had a relaxed air about him that was very soothing. Murder must be cathartic, stressful in the moment but afterward, what a release. I read someplace that the killing isn't so hard, but the disposal of the body is a major workout. That explains why most serial killers aren't fat turds, like your standard pedophile, but are usually fit and decent looking.

I went out to tan in my front yard one summer morning, not long after my ex had moved away. I had my ex's old walkman and some tapes and a pair of blue headphones so I could jam out while tanning. Rold saw me from across the street and lifted his hand, waving. It was hot, maybe too hot to be tanning, but I wore a new brown bikini, and I didn't mind if Rold, or anyone really, saw me in it. He was watering the marigolds and cosmos and sunflowers. I waved back at him and walked over.

"Hiya," he said. "Going out to work in your yard?"

He seemed to be suggesting that this was a good idea.

I pulled a petal off of a flower and sniffed it. "The neighbor boy said he'd mow it next week."

Rold studied me quietly. I had unthinkingly put the petal in my mouth and was now chewing it. I quickly scooped the wet wad out from under my tongue and flicked it onto the lawn.

"So," I said. "How's the gardening? Enjoyable?"

"It's not even that I enjoy it," Rold said. "What I enjoy is watching the cycle of life: things being born, giving fruit, returning to the earth."

I nodded. I understood where he was going with all of this. "My favorite part is when it's all over," I said. I was trying to call his bluff. "You know, the death part of it all."

Rold laughed. It was a gorgeous, wonderful sound. I could see the silver fillings in his teeth. I wanted to wrap my arms around him and tickle him so the golden sound would fill the air around us. My ex rarely laughed, and when he did it seemed as though he was stifling himself, as though he didn't want to appear too happy around me. Seeing Rold laugh with such abandon lifted my spirits. Here was a man that I had delighted, and he was happy to share his delight with me.

Still chuckling, Rold wandered over to the side of his house and shut off the water. The water stopped with one last lurch of the hose. I surveyed the garden. The wet leaves glittered like coins in the sun.

"Do you wear cologne?" I asked. The reason I asked this was because the smell of the petal and its bitter taste were still lingering in my nose and mouth. It just got me thinking about smells, is all.

Rold shook his head and said, "You certainly know how to keep a man on his toes."

I brushed the sole of my bare foot across the recently mown grass and shivered, it felt so good. Then I nodded at the owl. "She's a real beaut."

Rold winked. "She's a 'He."

I was surprised at that. I had always assumed it was an owl woman. "He stares at my house."

Rold smiled and started wrapping up the hose in a neat coil. "He's like you. He's vigilant." Rold gazed at me for a moment and then added, "Maybe he likes what he sees."

40

"I hope so," I said. "Well, I better get back to my tanning."

I glanced through Rold's windows as I ambled back to my yard. Cluttered on a squat coffee table were the backs of what looked like silver picture frames. I pictured my face in every one of them: pensive, surprised, smiling.

•

After my ex left and when I couldn't sleep, I would spy on Rold's house, watching for any suspicious behavior. One night he returned home late, almost three in the morning, with what was undoubtedly a hooker. She was really tall, wearing three-inch blocky heels and a white fur. She was also smashed out of her gourd. She kept leaning on the fence, wavering there like a ghost, saying, "Baby. I don't feel so good. Whoa, the train's a comin' babe. Hold my hair back in case. Be a gentleman, babe." She barfed in the garden twice.

Rold petted her back and glanced around the street. This wasn't going well, I thought. Any other neighbor might have been on the phone with the cops already. But he did manage to coax her into the house. At sunrise, I awoke to the sounds of a door slamming, and I went to the window to see Rold holding a glossy black garbage sack, standing behind his SUV and wiping the sweat from his brow with the back of his pale, spidery hand. It was early and the shadows were thick, but I could make out dark patches of what had to be blood on his jeans. He had done what any sensible serial killer would do: get the chick drunk, get her in his bathtub, chop her up into a dozen pieces. He hoisted the sack into the trunk with a loud grunt and then drove away. I thought of following him but knew I couldn't pedal my bike fast enough.

A few weeks later Rold heaved open his garage door and backed his black SUV out into the street. He reserved this car for special occasions. I knew he would be gone until much later in the evening.

I went across the street in the dark, wearing only my silk robe, no panties and no bra. It was like swimming nude in cold water: liberating. I opened the small gate to his yard and padded across the cold grass. I was in bare feet and the perfectly grown spears of his lawn brushed sweetly against my soles. I could see the unimpressive profile of the owl, unimpressive because they have no noses and such short beaks. For the first time, I was staring at him instead of him staring at me. There was his spade, lying by the white cellar door. It was sparkling clean, despite having interred so many bodies, and it gleamed in the moonlight. I took the shovel into my hands and gripped it tightly. I shut my eyes and pictured hitting a home run and slammed the spade into the owl with all of my might. He peeled off of the fence and thudded onto the dirt below.

The air smelled like bruised basil and I breathed there for a moment and looked up at the moon. What did I look like from above, standing in this man's yard, holding a shovel in one hand, panting? I replaced the shovel against the cellar door and returned to the owl. It was surprisingly light, hollow. Cradling it to my breast, I exited back through the gate and sprinted across my yard and into my house.

In bed, I held the owl to my chest and sobbed a little sob of joy. Why does it feel so good to take things? To take lives, to take photographs, to take a ceramic owl. It would feel good to give, too, if there was anyone to give to, but that ship had sailed. My ex-boyfriend, before moving back to Seattle, warned me, "It is possible to be too giving, you know." I remembered that when I stole his old prized walkman – one of the few remaining in the land of iPods – on his last day with me.

I thought about the guy with the mountain bike and the power drill. These are utilitarian items. When he used them, he might ponder the serial killer's accomplishments: 1) Pedaling to a victim's house. 2) Lobotomizing someone. It would be satisfying to use them for cleaner purposes. For example: 1) Biking up the hillside to enjoy a nice sunset. 2) Building an entertainment center. Then you could compare yourself to the serial killer. You could say, "I have done something better and healthier with these objects." Or you could say, "Objects don't have brains or memories." You could say a lot of things, and they would probably be both right and both wrong. Like everything in life.

The owl was staring at the ceiling when I woke up the next morning, his body resting on the opposite pillow. Owls don't have chins, but if they did the blanket was tucked up to where it would be. Through the open window, I could hear Rold across the street saying, "Tut tut." I couldn't see him, but he might have been running his hand over the jagged portion of the fence where his owl had once perched. I pictured him crossing the street, knocking angrily on my door, spouting invectives until I emerged wearing my loveliest nightie. Then he would drink in the sight of me and I would say in a husky voice, "Please, Rold, come in." We would share a beer and talk things over. We would really open up to one another. I pictured a small private wedding in his garden. My face would glow from every one of his living room's silver frames. I would forgive him all of his wrongdoings. He would regard me like a saint.

I waited for the knock on my door but none came. It was too early to be awake after a murdering spree.

"Go back to sleep," I told the owl, patting the pillow. The owl rolled toward me, his wide yellow eyes fixed on my face. I heard the sounds of children playing somewhere, happy sounds that filled the street with squeals of companionship. "Don't cry you big baby," I told the owl. "You'll never be alone again." He continued to stare at me, terrified.

I was dozing when I heard a faint knock on the door. It barely roused me at first, but then I heard it again. I threw off of the covers and dressed quickly, calling "I'll be right there!" I combed my hair just enough so that it began to rise upward, buoyant with static. "Damn it," I said, but then I decided to leave it alone and let Rold see me for who I am. I raced to the door and opened it.

"Sarah," Rold said, not unkindly. "I think you have something that belongs to me."

His eyes were hidden behind wraparound sunglasses that ran in a parallel line to his blond strip of hair. The top of his head gleamed white in the sun. His mouth was upturned, amused. He kept his hands behind his back.

"Tut tut," he said, in a mild mocking tone, and then he entered my home, pushing gently by me. I shut the door. I felt a relaxation like I had never known. I stayed facing away from him. I looked outside at the young children running carefree in the street. Their bloodstreams carried no traces of cement yet, but as they grew older they would feel their bodies thicken. It made me happy to see them out there, so weightless and so free.

Rold said something from behind me. I shut my eyes and listened to the cries of the children. His arms went around me. He was laughing. He said he was also vigilant. He said he had seen me take his owl. One arm went around my throat. I brought my hands up and enfolded them around his forearm, the way a lover might. His muscles twitched wildly beneath my fingers. We went down to the floor this way; with me facing away from him. Pleasant bubbles of bright colors burst against my eyelids. He was kissing my cheek, the back of my neck. I heard nothing but my own blood washing over itself, coursing through me, the sounds of my interior mechanisms. The children were gone. I wanted to turn my head to look at him, but I was so blissfully tired. My head was in his lap. He released my throat and asked if I was comfortable. He massaged my neck, my shoulders. I heard my heartbeat resume, loudly.

"I'll take care of you," Rold said. "Relax." He began to unbutton my blouse.

"I am," I said. "I'm so happy." Tears sprang to my eyes. I was having trouble breathing. What if he didn't want me? What if I wasn't his type?

"You're perfect," my serial killer said. "You're so perfect."

And in those next few minutes, I was.

vvvvvvvvvvvvvvvvvvvvvvvvvvv

LYING DOWN

ΛΛΛΛΛΛΛΛΛΛΛΛΛΛΛΛΛΛΛΛΛΛΛΛΛΛΛ

1

We arrive at seven to drink coffee and chat with Sven. Sven will be an okay boss. He offers us donuts. He asks about our marriage. He says we look healthy. Dewey and I hold hands. Sven sits down on a mattress and bounces a little, but not too much. Ruins the springs, he says. He instructs us to move as little as possible.

"The key is," he says, "look happy. Look placated. No big shit-eating grins. Just smiles, like you're dreaming of money, or of sex, or of your favorite Grandma. Whatever makes you happy. Your kids. Do you have any kids?"

Dewey shakes his head. "We've tried," he says.

He squeezes my hand. The coffee is very bitter.

Sven strokes his chin. "No kids? I hope the customers don't sense that."

"Unless," I offer, "they are customers who don't want kids. Then they would want to sense that."

Sven brightens. "That's why I hired you. The smarts. The customers don't need to know you're childless. And if they ask, wing it. You can pretend you have them. This could be your sort of alternate marriage space, you know?"

"A marriage utopia," Dewey says. He squeezes my hand again.

I squeeze his hand, too. This will be a good job.

2

The doors open at eight. Dewey and I select a mattress that massages your spine. It feels so good I want to fall asleep. But we can't look slack-jawed and ugly. We're hired to sell, not to sleep, Sven says. I can hear people walking around in the mall outside. I open one eye and peek at Dewey. He is feigning sleep excellently, with a small smile on his face, all dimples and curly brown hair. He looks cute. I peck him on the cheek. Sven shouts, "Good! Good! Now back to sleep!" Dewey smiles bigger. "Too big!" shouts Sven. Footsteps sound outside of the door, crowds passing, maybe entering the "I Saw It on TV" store across from us, or the electronic store next door, where you can play computer games for free. I think I doze off for a moment, but then the massaging rollers vibrate me awake again.

At eleven, the first couple enters. Sven greets them, his voice high and eager. I turn over and stage a pleasant sigh. The couple notices. They walk up to the bed, chatting.

"Who are they?" asks the man.

"They are a happy couple, sleeping on this fine mattress," Sven replies. "The Reverberator Two-thousand. Vibrating rollers gently caress your muscles while stimulating the metabolism. Leaves you relaxed. Burns fat. Excellent for tonage."

"Tonage?" says the woman.

"Muscle tonage."

"They look happy," says the man.

I'm so happy, I want to tell him.

"What's the price?" the woman asks.

Sven tells them. The woman gives a little laugh. "Steep," she chirps. "Steep, steep."

"Well, it's a lotta bed," Sven says. He's good at sounding both timid and pushy.

The couple wanders around a little more, finally selects a Dreamcatcher, extra firm.

When they leave, Sven lets us take a break. He claps Dewey on the back. "Excellent work, kids," he says. "I think you two will be a goldmine for me."

Dewey's brow furrows. He leans forward to take another donut. "Yeah," he says, "but they didn't buy the one we were sleeping on."

I speak before Sven does. "I think we inspired them. I think we looked so happy that they thought, wow, let's get a mattress right now."

Sven nods. "See, that's why I hired you. The smarts. Alright, kids, go lie down on the Reverberator Two-thousand. Make it look comfy."

Dewey and I hold hands all the way to the bed. I am having great fun. Dewey and I stretch and yawn. We make a big show. A woman with lipstick bloodying her teeth comments on how much she likes my silk pajamas. Where did I get them? I tell her in the mall, at the opposite end, borrowed from SleepWare, Etc. I lie down. Dewey and I fall into instant fake sleep. The massagers roll up and down my back. I think I'm actually sore from lying on them all morning, but I smile slightly anyway. I pretend-dream of a big fat baby boy. I pretend-dream that Dewey holds him on his knee in a bright, spic-and-span kitchen. He bounces him up and down, in rhythm to the pounding of the massagers. I almost fall asleep as Sven discusses prices. The woman ambles around the store. She purchases a Dreamcatcher, extra firm.

No other customers.

Sven will be a good boss. He gives us a fifty-dollar, first-day bonus, and also the box of donuts. Dewey holds the box on his lap during the bus ride home. We eat the donuts for dinner.

3

On payday, I call Mom. "Long time no word," she says.

"I'll call more now." I wash the silverware while we talk. There are never any dishes to wash. We use paper plates. I tell her, "Dewey and I have a steady income."

"'Bout time. Mattresses, eh? Moving out of that dump?"

"No," I say. I hear screaming in the background. "We're saving for doctor appointments."

"For the babies?"

"Mom, what is that screaming?" A piece of dried cereal is stuck to a fork.

"For the babies?"

"Yes, for babies."

"It's the TV," she says. "William's watching it. TURN IT DOWN!" she shrieks. "Listen," she says, "could you pick up one of those electric hair removers for me from 'I Saw It on TV'? I need one…TURN IT DOWN! for the lobes on William's ears. And maybe for the part above his nose. Maybe for my legs? How about it? An early Christmas present?"

"Mom, I'm saving money."

"For babies." Mom sighs.

"How are you feeling?"

"Babies would be good. Couple a kids. We could fly up." She shrieks, "TURN IT DOWN FOR CHRIST'S SAKE!" Then, "I'm fine, sweetie. Tired. Medicine swells me up. Suffering from lethargia. Doctor says it's normal, otherwise my ticker's shipshape."

"Alright, Mom," I say, "That's good. I just wanted to say 'hi.' That I love you both. Tell William."

"You like your job?"

"Yeah," I say. "It's easy. But it's getting harder to sleep. I get bored lying down."

"Huh. You'll adjust. Try sleeping propped up in the shower. William does. Or in a Lazy-Boy, he does that too. Or leaning on the rake in the yard, when you're supposed to be raking leaves. William –"

"Maybe I'll try. Well, I gotta go, Mom. Costing money. Talk to you soon."

"Listen," she says, "is it inspiring?"

"Is what inspiring?"

"Lying side by side all day?"

"I don't know."

She coughs, mumbles something about the TV. "I mean, does it get things going for you two? In bed?"

"Mom, I don't know."

But I do know. What I know is that we had sex a couple of weeks ago, after the first day of work, after our donut dinner, but since then, not at all. But it's been awhile since we've worked all day. We'll break out of it once we adjust, as Mom says.

"Well, babies would be good," she says now, "good luck with that. Let me know if it happens."

We hang up. The silverware is clean, so I search the house for Dewey. He's in the bedroom, hands on hips, doing lunges. His eyes look heavy. We haven't been sleeping much.

"I'm trying to tire myself out," he says. "I'm getting fat."

"We lie around all day," I point out.

"Right."

"I like to be with you," I say.

"I like you, too."

He smiles and lunges, up and down, up and down.

4

After the second paycheck, we book an appointment. In the waiting room, a kid with a bad cold sneezes on Dewey. Dewey scowls. He's anxious about the baby. He hopes, right now, that I'm pregnant. He says I'm probably a month gone, he can tell by the flab around my belly button. I think maybe it's just flab, from eating donuts and lying around all day. But we're making money. We can book appointments.

In the doctor's office, Dewey's happier. He's sure she'll return with a thumbs-up sign. I enjoy his good mood while I can. I will be sad if it's my fault.

But it's not my fault. The doctor says to Dewey, "Mr. Ferver, I'm sorry to tell you that your sperm count is practically nil."

Dewey says, "Nil? As in, a mil?"

"No. Nil, as in nothing."

Dewey spaces out. He stares out the window.

"Is there a chance?" I ask. I give her a pleading look. I want her to say something positive, even if it's a lie, just to make Dewey stop spacing out.

"There's always a chance," she says, "about one in a million, but you never know."

"We could have sex a million times," Dewey suggests.

"Yes," she says, but she sounds hesitant.

Dewey says, "I know I have sperm. I've seen it. The white gunk? Where they swim around?"

The doctor says, "Mr. Ferver, don't feel guilty. There's no accounting for these things. You certainly didn't do anything for this to happen. It's just the way life goes."

We are speechless.

"But you can adopt," she suggests. She glances at her watch. "You can babysit."

I stand and take Dewey's hand. We leave without saying another word. I promise a second opinion. We get one, but the second doctor says the same.

"We can't adopt," Dewey says. "We're poor. They'd never give us a baby."

"We'll keep working," I say. "It'll be okay. There are other options."

"Those options are expensive." Dewey won't look at me when we speak. Right now, he mechanically rips up his paper plate and folds the pieces into miniature airplanes. Six or seven of them are lined up on the kitchen table, aimed at his chest. Sighing now, he stops folding and says, "We're poor. We're too poor. We're fucked."

Dewey never swears. I lean forward and gather the planes into my hand. "We'll just keep working." I pick up what's left of his plate and sweep everything into the trash. I get a fresh plate and ask, "Want a donut?"

Dewey shakes his head. "I need to lie down."

"Okay."

He goes in the bedroom and lies down. He gets up for work in the morning and then lies down. We get home and he lies down. Then he gets up for work and then lies down again. I can't sleep at all anymore, unless it's in the shower, propped up as my mother suggested. But even then it's hard. I'm uncomfortable everywhere.

A few weeks pass. Dewey looks gradually unhappier at work. Sven's confused. Mattresses aren't selling. Dewey won't talk to me, just stares. He thinks I'll leave him. I cuddle up to him at work, smiling slightly. I still dream of a big fat baby boy. On Dewey's knee. Dewey bounces him. The rollers pound into my spine. I'm used to the pain now, but there is no muscular tonage.

5

Sven pulls me aside. Dewey refuses to take a break. He remains lying prone on the mattress, his mouth slack. Sven says, "What's going on? Zombie over there is losing us business."

"He lost his manhood," I say. My voice breaks. I cry a little bit. Sven gets a Kleenex for me and pats me on the shoulder. When I blow my nose it honks like a bus braking.

"Jeez," he says.

He waits for me to explain, and when I do, he offers to help.

"Help how?"

"Well, you could come here after hours, without Dewey," he says. "We could practice lying down on the mattress. Just for a week or so. Problemo solved. Business saved."

I'm shocked at his suggestion, but I tell him I'll think about it. I go and lie down beside my husband. He mumbles something incoherently. Drool spills down his jaw.

"Listen," I say, "things are going to be okay."

He says, "No. We're fucked."

"Dewey," I tell him, "I had a dream that I was pregnant. And you know my dreams always come true? A big fat baby boy? And you, bouncing him on your knee?"

I don't tell him that it's a fake dream, one that I imagine when I'm fake-sleeping. Dewey turns toward me, pecks me between the eyes. I feel cross-eyed, looking at him this close.

"Really?" he asks.

I nod.

"Just stick with me," he says, happier now. "Things will work themselves out. You're gonna stick with me, right? Even though you really want kids?"

"Like glue," I say. "Don't worry."

I stay extra hours all week. Dewey goes home to pour cereal into our paper bowls. He waits for me to come home before he adds the milk. He doesn't even ask why I stay late.

6

It's the end of the week and Sven says to me, "That should do it."

We're lying on the Pegasus Mobile bed. I stuff my arms back into my shirt. There's a little TV that pops up at the foot of the bed, and Sven clicks it on.

"I hope I helped," Sven says sincerely.

I don't say anything. I pull on my jeans. A janitor passes by, his huge vacuum cleaner whirring. He spots us through the window. Sven waves him away.

"Want to watch something? *Singin' in the Rain?*" Sven asks.

I shake my head. "I'm tired," I say. "Dewey's waiting."

Sven shrugs and looks a little hurt. He's got funny, pinched features, but his eyes are friendly and warm. He's not so bad looking, but I can't stand his face, anyway.

"I appreciate it, though," I tell him. I don't want him to feel rotten, the way I do.

"I hope it helps," Sven says again, brightening. "That should do it, I think."

"Yeah," I say. "I hope so. I feel rotten enough as it is."

He shuts off the TV and the flickering stops. The fluorescent lights hum.

"I feel pretty rotten," I repeat.

"Don't," Sven says. "You're doing this for Dewey. For your marriage. An alternate marriage space, remember? I mean, you can pretend this never happened."

Dewey had said *Utopia*. I thank Sven, collect my things, and leave. Sven offers me a ride home, but I tell him no, the bus is fine, thanks.

7

At seven, Dewey and I hold our coffee cups. Sven cracks open the box of donuts. He avoids looking Dewey or me in the eye. I reach for Dewey's hand. He shakes my hand away. I select a chocolate éclair. Dewey eats an éclair, a powdered donut, a jelly-filled donut. He is about to pick up his fourth when Sven tells us, "Customers on deck. Head to the Vetro Elastabed." We head there. I stretch and yawn, make a big show. My heart is not in it. Out of the corner of my eye I see Dewey sloppily kick off his shoes, violently throw back the sheets. He flops onto the bed like a big dying porpoise. The customers, a tall woman in pink heels holding the hand of her short pale daughter, are startled. Sven frowns for only a moment. He raises his eyebrows to me, clasps the tall woman's elbow, and guides her to the bed. I continue putting on a big production. Sven looks grateful. I blink a few times, pretend that I can hardly keep my eyes open, and then let my lips part just enough so that my teeth don't show. Sven has said that my teeth are yellow like popcorn-flavored jellybeans. So now I'm careful.

Sven charms the woman. He explains the bed. The woman asks questions. He says, "This bed was developed by NASA." She says that her husband moves around too much at night. He says, "You can set a full glass of wine on one side of this bed and drop a bowling ball on the other. No spillage." She says that she feels stiff in the morning. Sven says, "Sleeping on metal springs? Thought so. Switch to foam. Switch to vetro-elastic memory cells. Any position, no stiffness." The woman goes quiet. She seems to be studying something, carefully. I feel her breath hitting me. I smell her lavender perfume. Cracking one eye open, I see that she is studying my husband. Her breasts heave above my face.

"He looks unhappy," she tells Sven.

"Him? No! He's just been sleeping, at home, on a metal-spring mattress."

"He looks like he's having a nightmare."

"No, no, it's just that the superlative firmness of this mattress is relieving certain pressure points, thereby seeming to create a grimace when actually he's – "

"Come on, Cynthia," the woman says, straightening. Cynthia has her thumb in her mouth. They execute a small half-circle, holding hands, and start for the door.

"Thank you for coming in!" Sven shouts after them. He never burns bridges. I roll over and watch them enter "I Saw It on TV." The girl picks up the Stomachkiller, a product that issues small electric shocks to help you lose weight. Instead of attaching the electrodes to her abdominal muscles, she jams them to her temples. The mother tosses her arms up and shrieks.

"Do you think those work?" Sven asks me, watching as the mother pulls the girl back onto her feet.

"The Stomachkillers?"

"Yeah."

"No," I say. "But wouldn't it be easier if they did?"

"Yeah," he says. He looks at Dewey. Dewey is dead asleep and drooling. He sleeps most of the time now. "Escapist," Sven mutters. He kicks at the base of the bed.

8

Today Sven tells us to lie on the Pegasus Mobilebed. This is the one bed I cannot stand lying on. I even like the Reverberator 2000 more. I have a hard time pretending to be asleep when things are vibrating, folding, flattening and flashing. It surprises me that this bed is a bestseller. Sven is very proud of it.

Strangely though, today I manage to fall asleep. I have still not been sleeping at night, although yesterday I did fall asleep while trying to mow the lawn in the dark. Dewey hollered at me through the bedroom window that I was going to kill myself that way. He didn't bother getting out of bed to tell me so. But today I fall asleep. I have a bad dream. In the dream, Dewey bounces a big fat baby boy on his knee. The baby has a moustache and a receding hairline. He has crows-feet and pointed ears. It is Sven's head, screwed onto a baby's body. I look at Dewey. He cries, silently, and when he meets my eyes I see how accusatory he is.

I wake up, screaming Dewey's name.

Dewey grabs me. The mattress buckles upward, under my knees. It slides like an eel beneath my spine. A customer jumps away from the mattress. He watches, at first confused, then just nosy, as Dewey cradles me and asks me over and over, "What's wrong, sweetums, what's wrong?"

All I can say is, over and over, "I'm sorry. I'm so sorry."

I think Sven will fire us. But he puts an arm around the customer's shoulders and walks him to another bed, across the store.

"Why?" Dewey asks me.

I am watching Sven. I say, "What?"

"What are you sorry for?"

I turn to Dewey. His eyes are big gooey gumballs, sugary with worry. I realize, suddenly. *He has no idea.*

"I'm sorry," I say. "I have to go to the bathroom."

I get sick in the bathroom. I puke all over. I start with the garbage can, continue with the sink, finish with the toilet. Chunks fall on my borrowed silk slippers, on the foot of my borrowed silk robe. Sven hears me gasping. He finishes a sale and then cleans up for me. I shudder and cough. I cannot get control of myself. Sven asks me to please calm down. He asks is there anything he can do. I can't even look at him. I want him to take it all back. He asks again. I cry harder. He says he is ashamed. He wants to apologize. I cannot accept. I tell him someone must accept my apology first. He starts to say something else, but Dewey knocks on the door.

I change and go home early. Without Dewey. Without donuts.

9

Sven lays me off. He says he can only afford one of us now, with Christmas coming. He has gifts to buy, he says. But he arranges a new job for me at "I Saw It on TV." Since they are a chain, they have benefits. And I get to walk around all day. My legs slim down some, but my stomach keeps growing. With my new discount, I buy Mom the Nyethair Russian-electrical-hair-removal system. I will send it to her for Christmas.

Dewey saves up some money and buys real dishes. There's more to wash, but I feel special eating cereal beside him at night, in real ceramic bowls. I can eat three bowls of cereal now and chug two glasses of milk. Dewey watches me, shocked but excited. Sometimes he urges me on. I'll barely finish before he'll rise and pour me a fresh batch. I haven't told him yet, but he guesses. I'll go to the doctor soon, for vitamins and such. Eventually I'll call Mom.

He's a lot happier, Dewey is. He does his lunges again, and he's slimmer. The other day he lifted my shirt and looked impressed with my larger breasts. He said he felt manly again. I said, yes, you should.

In the evenings, I walk across the orange mall hallway, as large as a four-lane road, to meet Dewey and catch the bus. I wave at Sven through the window. Sometimes they have last-minute business to wrap up. Tonight I see Dewey curled up in front of an elderly couple. I see him pretend-mumbling in his fake sleep, a tiny smile on his face. The couple kisses one another, speaks a few words to Sven, produces a credit card. Something shifts in my gut. I put my hands over my stomach and hold my breath.

Dewey jogs outside, pulling on his jacket. "Ready to go?" he asks. He is happy, smiling. He hugs me. I hug him back.

We turn together, down the vast hallway. The janitor glances up at us as we pass. He's struggling with the huge vacuum cleaner, trying to get it to start. I look down at the marmalade carpet where the day's detritus waits to be cleared away. Dewey reaches for my hand, squeezes.

"Steaks tonight, okay?"

"Okay," I say.

Life is improving.

BRAINS AND BEAUTY

I was almost seven when Medusa turned my brother to stone.

Bernard and Medusa were roughly the same age, ropey nine-year-olds who ran, swam and spoke much faster than I did. Medusa could be aloof and austere, but Bernard was a cruel boy by nature. He relished torturing Medusa's snakes, whether by pulling on them or tying them in heavy knotted loops. He even fed one of the snakes an atomic fireball, causing the poor thing to thrash about so wildly that I worried it would die right there on top of her head. For her part, Medusa handled Bernard's abuse gracefully, with little more than a small exhalation of annoyance, as though Bernard were merely a vague responsibility of hers, a clueless dog or hamster that had innocently shat on her shoe. I admired her forbearance.

The day of "the accident" (as my parents would call it, whenever they could bring themselves to mention it), I was trailing after Bernard and Medusa in the yard that connected our two homes, vaguely hoping to garner some of their attention, violent or no. My efforts, as usual, were failing. With the loyalty of passionate lovers, my brother and his playmate only attacked one another. It was a bizarre sort of tunnel vision into which I could never penetrate.

Bernard, on this particular occasion, decided to intensify Medusa's affliction, and leaned forward to bite a snake where it writhed from her skull. Medusa, with a cry of pain and anger, turned on him. Her green eyes flashed red. Right there, only a foot or so away from me, his body froze. Within moments, his flesh and clothing took on a flinty limestone veneer, so that he closely matched my mother's cement birdfeeder. Medusa, horrified, fluttering with apologies, tried to massage his arms and face back to mobility, but nothing worked. He was now what he would be forever. A statue. A harmless thing. Tripping over myself with excitement, I ran to my parents' house to tell them the bad news.

Bernard was my parents' favorite child – a fact that I never fully understood nor accepted. He was a runt, with the jagged buckteeth of a rabid beaver and ears that pointed away from his head as though determined to fly off and away. His hair was a dusty brown – unremarkable – while mine was ivory-blonde, the hair of a fairy princess. I, for one, knew I was a beautiful child. My earliest memories told me so. My parents' friends exclaimed over me, even perfect strangers at the grocery store. I blinked up at these looming faces and listened with some rapture to their compliments about my face, my eyes, my skin, *that gorgeous hair!* My parents smiled, thin-lipped and polite, but they were modest God-fearing folk who frowned on vanity and preferred awkwardness, so they offered no endorsement. Yes, they admitted, I was lovely. That was that.

My brother, on the other hand, was deemed reckless and wild by these same friends and strangers. He was the sort of child that ran amuck wherever he went, spilling books from their shelves at the library or upending a stack of fruits at the grocery store. When our mother pulled him away from some such deviance, he threw a vicious, loud temper tantrum that placed great strain on the faces of all employees and civilians nearby. *A spirited boy*, the kindest of their friends said. *Creative*, suggested another. To this, my parents were quick to respond about my brother's singular genius, that Bernard was *terribly* intelligent – too intelligent, really, to be expected to behave himself at all hours of the day. *Imagine being so intelligent and so young*, they lowed. *How frustrated he must get! Because, like all geniuses, he's a perfectionist.* These statements baffled me. I wondered why it was so preferable to be a destructive genius than to be a mannerly beauty. At the dinner table, I watched, annoyed, as he was gently coaxed into eating a mere bite of whatever disgusting food I had already, against my will, obediently devoured. I both loved him and hated him. I both sought his approbation and longed for his demise. In return, Bernard treated me with his own special brand of cruelty, ignoring me for long hours until some whininess on my part would provoke him to take the downy skin of my forearm between his thumb and forefinger and twist until the tears sprang up in my eyes.

And so it was with some delight, with some feverish evil relish, that I sprinted into my parents' kitchen and called for them to come quickly, to come see what Medusa had done to poor Bernard.

There had been, of course, the expected urgings to sue the Gorgons, my parents' neighbors, for turning their son into a pillar of stone, but my parents were sensible and kind by nature, and they agreed with the Gorgons that what had transpired was merely a horrible accident – a childhood play date gone terribly awry. Nonetheless, after several months of deep effort, despite all of their good-natured, well-meaning intentions, my parents ultimately could not stand the sight of the snake-haired girl, nor could they stomach her apologizing, clumsy, impoverished parents, and so we moved away from Spokane to Seattle, where my father found work as an architect's assistant.

Bernard remained with us, firmly secured in the backyard not far from the matching cement birdfeeder, his stone sneakers rooted firmly into a patch of dirt that Mom decorated with tulips and irises, his cruel little face wearing its perennial pursed, teasing expression. Every morning, rain or shine, Mom sent me out to scrub off the guano and pollen from his marble frame. Sometimes, when bored, I would play with him, dressing him up in my own clothes until my parents, irritated, ordered me to stop. At night, in bed, I thought about Medusa with a restless gratefulness, anxious for the sadness of my parents but relieved that Bernard was now harmless. By turning my brother to stone, she had saved me countless hours of taunting and torture and terror. An added benefit, too, was that I was now, despite his omnipresence in the grass, the only child. I received the near total of my parents' affection and financial support.

Medusa, herself, briefly garnered the attentions of a local ensemble of scientists, and as the years passed my family read studies of her in various scientific magazines, and finally in a book, *Field Guide to Monsters of the Inland Northwest*, in which the author devoted an entire chapter to her behaviors and talents. By the time of its publication, I was a senior in high school, having just been accepted into a prestigious college elsewhere in the country. (*Brains and beauty*, my parents' friends gushed. *You're so lucky to have such an upstanding young lady in the household*.) Medusa, however, never completed high school, but with the help of a patient tutor had finally managed to secure a GED. She was uncertain of what she would do next in life, but she planned to stay in Spokane, mostly because she lacked money and prospects elsewhere. Aside from being able to turn people to stone (which she had only done once, with unfortunate Bernard), she had nothing more to contribute to society. That was all we learned before the scientists grew bored of her and the publications ceased. My parents, kindly people that they were, mentioned that they almost felt sorry for her. In a way, her own life was frozen, as Bernard's had been.

"I wonder if we should call her," I said, moved by their pity. "Or write her a letter."

My mother shuddered.

"That's not necessary," my father said sharply. "We've moved on and so should she."

I let my suggestion die, seeing how deeply it mortified them. I should have known better. Any disagreeable statement delivered them afresh to their woe. I frequently came upon them weeping together in the kitchen, their arms around one another, sharing a private pain to which I was uninvited.

College proved to be a happy diversion from the woes of my family, and sometimes I forgot about Medusa and Bernard and my pained parents entirely. There was studying to be done, and drinking, and lovemaking, some of them more rewarding and enjoyable than others. Despite the mildly hedonistic lifestyle I lead, I graduated with distinction, and then went on to medical school, and became, of all things, a boring old dentist. It just so happened that an extremely well-paying job opened up in Spokane, and I accepted it immediately, lured by the affordable housing and proximity to lakes and to the memories of multiple sunny days in a row, a characteristic that Seattle had greatly lacked. As expected, I visited my parents in my moment of transitioning.

I was disturbed to find that they had dragged Bernard out of the yard and had placed him next to the fireplace in the living room. He stared cruelly at me as my parents and I gathered on the old familiar sofas. The three of us chatted inanely as people do when they don't know what to say to one another. The mood in the house was awkward. Every now and again my mother would turn to Bernard as if he were about to speak, her eyes shining and desperate. When he gave no response, she withdrew into the sad recesses of her mind. To encourage her reawakening, I leaned forward and touched her knee and told her some humorous story from my college years. Her eyes would flit over to me again, where I sat happy and lovely, vibrant and full-grown, so contrary to the short statue of her little boy, and she would smile vaguely, as if reading some bad joke on my face. I began to wonder if she was losing her mind. When I mentioned this later, in private, to Dad, he frowned at me angrily and said that they had been through quite a lot in their life, and would I mind terribly giving them some peace and quiet? After all, he said, no parents like to feel like their kid is judging them.

I said, no, that I wouldn't mind, and that I was sorry if he felt judged. He apologized to me for snapping and then confessed to me softly that sometimes, in the recent years since I'd left home, they'd imagined that Bernard had moved. After such a suspicion, they could no longer keep him in the yard. Every day they watched him for more movement.

"And has there been any?" I asked, silencing the judging part of my brain.

Dad shrugged. "Sometimes," he said, "it would seem so." Apparently the movement was too faint to be sure.

Equipped with this troubling news, I was relieved to escape their dark cheerless home. I was eager to begin my new career in Spokane. I insisted that my parents visit me when they could, and sometimes they did, and sometimes they even seemed happy and proud. I could not bear, however, to visit them. I could never shake the disturbing idea of Bernard being alive. One last night in my childhood bed, I dreamed that he slowly walked into my room – breathing shallowly – and put his cold, stone palm over my mouth and nose to suffocate me. After that, I decided – for my own mental health – that I couldn't return. If my parents were upset by this, they said nothing. They seemed all too pleased to visit me, instead. Perhaps they were even grateful. They might very well have loathed how visibly I doubted their hope.

As for Medusa, we had heard nothing about her since the publication of the now out-of-print book. When I brought up the question of her whereabouts, my father suggested dully that for all they knew, she might be dead. I felt a twinge of sadness at the coldness of his comment.

Meanwhile, my career and private life in Spokane blossomed healthily, as things do when you keep your desires modest and steady. I met a man who was also a dentist, an equally boring and sweet fellow with the teeth of a thoroughbred. We married in a small ceremony that made Mom cry with joy. My parents had brought Bernard, too, standing him stiffly in a suit and tie at the front of the chapel so that he joined the other groomsmen as we exchanged vows. I tried to ignore him as best as I could, but he was so immensely out of place. Not only was he made of stone, but he was also the only little-boy groomsman. For the first time, I thought about how he had been robbed of an entire life. His face seemed less taunting now, more solemn. His shadowy presence dimmed the brightness of my big day.

For the reception we placed him near the punchbowl with a glass of neon pink punch suspended in one hand. Dad joked that he was drinking too much. I hoped, nestled somewhere within all of that stone, that some part of Bernard's brain was enjoying itself.

A month or so after our honeymoon, a weird, embattled looking woman approached me in the parking lot of the dental offices where both my husband and I worked. She seemed part reptile – her face covered in scales and her hair floating over her head with what appeared to be a great amount of static. As she came closer, I saw indeed that she was reptilian, and that her hair was standing on end not because of static but because it was alive with thousands of electric strands of snakes.

"Medusa," I said. I was not cruel but warm, and her expression was surprised. I even offered her a hug, which she accepted awkwardly.

"You *are* Bernard's sister, right?" She stepped away from my embrace, her lidless green eyes searching mine.

I said that yes, indeed I was, and how was she doing nowadays?

"Oh, you know," she said. "Could be worse."

Looking at her, I didn't think so. She had always been famously ugly, of course, but I had, in fact, found her enviable as a child. She had been strong and vivid and funny. Not at all someone you wanted to avoid. But now she looked like a thing overcooked. Dry and shredded and weak. Her voice was very hoarse. She wore a shabby man's tank top and a pair of soiled slacks. Her arms hung from her body like two worn strips of leather. When we had embraced, her slightness had startled me. Like hugging a small featherless bird.

"It's been some years, and I wanted to say," she began. Her speech was uneducated, halting. "To apologize – to say how sorry I really am – for what I did to you all. To your brother. I never forgot – I tried to, for sure – but I never forgot. It's on my mind all the time. More than all the time." She stopped here, laughing at herself. "Every time! Every time I do anything, up it comes."

"But, Medusa," I said, gently chiding her, not wanting to make the moment too heavy, "you've already been forgiven. Don't you remember?"

She strained here for the memory, her nose wrinkling. "Maybe I do. A little. But I was so young. I don't believe it. I'm not forgiven, I'll bet."

I shook my head. "Believe me now, then," I said, feeling very charitable and kind, feeling like a wonderful sort of person. "You *are*. By everyone. By all of us. I'm only sorry that you had to go through all of this alone. It must have been terribly rough for you."

She seemed confused by my turning the apology around in such a way. "That's okay," she stammered. And then she fell silent. She seemed to be drinking in every word. Then, brightening, she lifted her face to me. "Thank you."

"It's nothing."

She started to slide away from me. I called her back. "Here," I said, and brought out a small amount of cash from my pocketbook. "You look like you might need a little help."

"Oh no," she said. "I couldn't. Gosh, you're really kind. I always remembered that. You being nicer. Nice, I mean."

I forced the bills into her hand and she finally accepted them, and we went our separate ways. I felt very proud of myself and even gloated about it to my husband over a plate of shrimp and rice. He said he was happy for me, and even happier for her. No doubt she would be able to pull herself together now and go on to do great things.

The next day, however, she met me in the parking lot again. She had thought over what I had said. She was certain that it couldn't be true.

"It's true," I reassured her. "I promise you. You *are* forgiven. I was being utterly sincere yesterday."

Medusa wore the same simple, scanty outfit today, despite a slight chill in the air. She rubbed at her temples as if fighting off a headache. "This is some sort of trick," she said. "A trick. I'm sure of it. I don't mean to sound mean. I know you're nice. But I feel it right here," she touched her sternum. "I'm not forgiven."

"Listen to me," I said, stooping down so that our eyes met level to level. A dangerous act to perform with a gorgon, but I was committed to saving her dignity. "It's true. I wouldn't lie about something so very important. I have forgiven you. My parents have forgiven you. You only need to forgive yourself."

We stood in the parking lot for several minutes. I repeated again and again my reassurances until her shoulders relaxed and she began nodding like a convert. Then I gave her a little money again and she walked off, seemingly satisfied.

But then she appeared again, the following afternoon. This time my husband was with me. I frowned a little when I saw her, but tried to buoy my spirits by reminding myself that I had done so very well in life, and that she had not, encumbered as she was by years and years of guilt. Again, she expressed doubt in my words, that I couldn't possibly be so generous, and that she was certain that my parents did not agree with me. I argued with her as cheerfully as I could. My husband watched our little conversation with mild interest. Finally, after bantering back and forth, I hyperbolized my parents' opinions of her to such a degree that Medusa had no choice but to listen to me.

"They think you're a *wonderful* person," I told her. "I spoke to them just last night. They wished me to convey to you how marvelous a girl they found you to be, so bright and funny. Why, my mother even said that you should give up the ghost, so to speak, and forget about them. Onward! That's what she said. Whatever happened was just as much Bernard's doing as your own. Although no one, you realize, was to blame, exactly. It was a misfortune. All of that aside, we all agree that you were and continue to be a wonderful person with a bright future."

Lies, of course – I had, indeed, spoken to my parents the night before, but I had not at all mentioned my recent dealings with their son's murderess. Nonetheless, they were powerful lies, and she quickly fell under their spell. She blinked up at me, reptilian mouth agape. She was floored by the transcendent ideas I proposed, by the flowery language. She stammered, touched her heart again, stamped her feet in their dirty shredded shoes. Eventually, overcome, she apologized profusely for bothering me, and thanked me for my kindness. She left this time with no financial boon.

"She's crazy," my husband said as we buckled ourselves into my car.

"She's struggling," I said. "Imagine. The years and years of guilt."

"You might need to get a restraining order."

"The poor thing is crippled by the past. What a shame. Despite it all, Bernard continues to terrorize her."

"She's stalking you," my husband said. "Frankly, I'm concerned."

I told him he was being silly. I went to bed that night forgetting all about it. I was confident in my most recent speech. She could hardly doubt my sincerity. I had given her such an overwhelmingly emotive performance.

She was not there the next day. I thought we were done. I told my husband and he said he was relieved.

But the following afternoon, she approached me again. She ran up to me, panting, and clutched my arm with her clawed fingers. I feared that she would draw blood.

"Give me your parents' phone number, so I can call them myself," she said.

This I would not do. I shook her scaled manacles off of me, drawing away from her, away from my car. She clawed at me, screaming. Such a horrible scream. She needed closure, Damn it, and why would I not offer it to her? It suddenly occurred to me that she might turn me to stone, too. I kept my eyes trained on the ground and slowly backed away from her toward the hissing sliding doors of the office building.

"All I want to know," she demanded, "is if *they* forgive me. *They* are his parents. *They* hate me. I'll die without knowing," she wailed. "Let me speak to them."

"You aren't well," I said. "You need help."

"I had a baby," she babbled, almost incoherent at this point, she was so upset. She had grabbed hold of my blouse to prevent me from escaping. "I had a baby. He was killed. So I know. I know what they feel. I know how much they hate me. You're just his sister. You're useless."

A cop arrived then. Someone in the office – my husband, as I found out later – had called them after seeing us struggle through the window. He, too, arrived on the scene, pulling Medusa away from me, telling her to calm down.

The cop apparently knew her. He rolled his eyes and called her a troublemaker. "One of our regulars downtown," he cracked to me with a sideways grin. He shackled her wrists while another cop arrived to take down my story.

I told them everything, shaking. I was afraid for myself and afraid for my parents.

"Did she threaten to harm you in any way?" the cop finally asked.

"Most certainly," I said. "She killed my brother, you know. I think she was here to kill me, too."

The man's eyebrows rose. He asked me to continue, drawing out details of how she had threatened me. I was not kind in my report. In fact, I exaggerated Medusa's statements, made it sound like my life had been dangling on the very precipice, which, in my defense, perhaps it had been. My husband, standing by my side with his hand against my back, egged me on, adding his own exaggerations. It was easier to fib with someone corroborating my story.

"My wife would be dead if you hadn't had showed up," my husband said urgently. "And yes, we would like to press charges."

By the end of our statement, the cops were cracking jokes about Medusa's hideousness. They would be taking her to jail, one of the cops commented, as she had apparently been skipping out on her parole. She would be in jail for a long time, they mused, because she never had anyone to pay her bail.

Soon thereafter, we went to court and got a restraining order. She sat there in the courtroom blinking vapidly. She seemed not to notice that we were there at all. A few months later, a social worker called to let us know that Medusa had been released from jail the day before. I said, "Okay, thanks," and started to hang up the phone. The social worker said, "Wait, there's more," and told me that Medusa had since been killed, struck dead by a train near Latah Creek only this morning. I was ashamed to feel relief at the news.

Not long after this occurrence, my parents called, rejoicing, to say that Bernard had moved again. Not only moved, but melted.

"Melted?"

"Yes," Dad said gleefully. "The stone just melted like butter onto the floor. First the left hand and now the entire arm. The doctors think he'll be himself again in a week."

"Wow," I said. I tried to gather up some excitement but my voice was hollow. "That's amazing."

"You'll get your brother back! Think of that!"

I thought of it. I thought of it all that day and all that evening. I went to bed, trying to seem excited about it to my husband, but it was all phony. I thought of all the times I'd whispered to his statue that I was glad he wasn't alive. That he was a bully. A jerk. What if he'd been awake all of that time, dormant but perceptive? What would he tell my parents when the stone melted from his lips?

My sister's a monster. Not Medusa. My sister. My sister.

This was the night I had the dream again. The dream about the stone hand coming down over my nose and mouth. This time the hand was flesh.

vvvvvvvvvvvvvvvvvvvvvvvvv

ANTROPOLIS

∧∧∧∧∧∧∧∧∧∧∧∧∧∧∧∧∧∧∧∧∧∧∧∧∧

My hatred for Agnes led directly to our family's appearance on *Oprah*. You'd say, oh, you didn't hate her; she was just your older sister. But she was not my older sister. She looked older, but I was the elder by two years. No matter. People thought she was prettier, older, smarter. It didn't matter that I got better grades, that I was three classes ahead of her. It didn't matter, for example, that the Antropolis was my idea.

Everyone credited Agnes with the Antropolis, even my parents and Uncle Hayward, but I made it up one night as I read *Kid's Life* with a penlight under my covers. I lifted a corner of the blanket so I could see Agnes where she sat cross-legged on my bedroom floor, braiding her long hair.

I said, "You know what's a good idea, Agnes?"

"What, Hannah?"

"If we made ant farms and sold them for twice as much money."

She wrinkled her nose, disgusted. "Ants are grody."

Grody. That was her word, direct quote. But the next day she was telling Uncle Hayward all about it. He had arrived recently from the city to settle what he called "rambunctious nerves." He thought the ants were a brilliant idea. He ordered the kits, which included special soil and food, a thin plastic farm, and about twenty-five Western-Harvester ants per purchase. He opened one door of our four-door garage and for days we swept and organized. He read us the directions for taking care of the ants, and even though I understood them from the get-go, Agnes had him repeat everything at least three times.

"But why do they die so fast?" she whined. She didn't like that the ants only lived a month or so in the farms, and I admit I didn't like it either, but while I understood this as merely a fact of life, Agnes was practically slitting her wrists over it.

"Without a queen," Uncle Hayward said, "they just don't live as long."

From where I stood next to the garage's chest freezer, I sighed and scratched at my elbow. Hayward was my favorite uncle, but he could be so annoyingly patient with Agnes.

He continued, "The company that we order the ants from doesn't permit us to order queens."

"But why not?" Agnes continued, even though he'd already explained this earlier that week.

"Because, stupid," I said, "they might run rampant and then cause severe ecological damage." I was good at quoting pamphlets directly. It was a photographic trait that drove my teachers and peers nuts. "Like fire ants, for example, or killer bees in Texas."

Hayward patted my head in a way that made me feel less smart than I sounded. "Maybe if you girls learn something from these ant-kits, you can start digging up your own ants and find a queen, yourselves."

I liked this idea. I foresaw huge glimmering dollar signs. "Don't order any more ants," I told Hayward. "I'll supply the ants from now on."

At first, our parents were skeptical of the whole ant farm idea. Hayward argued for us.

"It's a great summer project. The girls will learn a ton."

Though Dad respected Hayward as a businessman, he questioned his rationality. "I don't want ants all over my garage," he growled.

"There *are* ants all over your garage. Only these ants will be in tightly-sealed cases."

Dad shook his head.

Hayward pressed, "Don't you want the girls to learn fiscal responsibility? Customer-service relations? Respect for God's creatures?"

Dad harrumphed.

Mom said to him, "What do you care, Brett? You're never home anyway."

Dad sold medical equipment to hospitals all over the nation. He was making us, as Mom often said, "rich but unfulfilled." Mom, herself, believed that parenting consisted of greeting us after school and sitting with us on the couch while she stared glassy-eyed at the television. She wanted us to benefit from the womanly genius of Oprah, the only black person Mom had ever regarded seriously, aside from a kid named Eldridge that I had met at Jolly Cheezers and had played with in the ball crawl. The whole way home from Jolly Cheezers, Mom had applauded herself for not being a racist. "I was *happy* you were playing with that child," she told me. "I was *ecstatic*." She glowed over dinner and told Dad the whole story, too, and he said, "Good for you, Martha, good for you." This was always the encouragement he gave her when his mind had wandered elsewhere.

But yes, there was Oprah, and Mom would talk to us about the virtues discussed on the show, and then there was Springer, and Mom would tsk-tsk and sigh and tell us how pitiable these lower class people could be (*the poor things have never learned a modicum of morality. I mean, they have no time to think of such things*). Despite her disgust, I don't think Agnes bleeding from her ears on the couch would have torn Mom's eyes away from the brutality of that television set. I also believe, at the time, that she thought Springer was a hottie. Once he had embraced a pear-shaped, middle-aged woman not unlike herself, who was weeping because her husband had cheated on her yet again. With a passionate gasp, Mom sank her fingers into my forearm. When she let go, there were long white claw marks where the blood used to be. I was hoping that these would turn into bruises so that I could tell the school counselor the next day. Maybe I would get invited to the Springer show myself. Or even better, because it would destroy my mother, Oprah would call and ask me to share my dreadful experiences with her. But within minutes my arm was back to normal.

At first, Mom gushed about how Uncle Hayward's appearance in the house would be "absolutely grand." I think she assumed he would take her side on all things, especially where her husband was concerned. But while Hayward doted on Agnes and me, he gave my parents little attention. "Your concerns are your concerns," he told my mother, and when she retorted that his involvement with the Antropolis idea was "a stupid, horrible sign of how horribly immature" he always had been and still very much was, Uncle Hayward just laughed. Dad didn't seem to mind Hayward's presence so much, although sometimes he muttered things like, "Hayward seems more than a little off," and "What sort of a man doesn't enjoy beer?" These statements arrived at odd moments, like when he was shaving, or when he sitting by himself with the newspaper. They were always said to no one in particular. Mom said that Dad's talking to himself was the surest sign of his megalomania.

The week before school ended, Agnes and I went around the hallways taping up hand-scrawled flyers advertising "The Antropolis!!!" I had come up with the name after rifling through hundreds of variations: Anttastic, Ant You Happy, Ants in Your Pants. Agnes had come up with one lousy name, "Antsville," which Hayward feigned to like until I belted out, *Antropolis!* Agnes started crying. Hayward patted her back and said things like, "She wouldn't have thought of it if you hadn't said 'Antsville,'" which was a total lie, and that "Those who succeed stand upon the shoulders of giants," which made her a giant and me a total shrimp. I saw an ant glide beneath me on the cool pavement. I put my foot to it and wiped its guts into a sweeping frown. "Is it *Antropolis* or not?" I asked. Hayward nodded at me but also put a finger to his lips. I stomped into the house. Later, prompted by Hayward, Mom visited me in my room and told me not to be upset by his giving Agnes more attention. "She's younger than you and more sensitive," Mom said. But what she meant was "She's stupider than you and more attractive." I told Mom to stuff it and thus martyred myself out of a fried-chicken dinner. Dad snuck a piece to me later. He knew it was my favorite.

The week after school finished, we had a flurry of customers. The neighborhood mothers found Hayward handsome, and they couldn't wait to sidle up to him, stroking the pearls that grew like pale tumors from their necks and wrists, and purr about what a "deliciously adorable thing" he'd done, helping darling Agnes and that ("What's her name again? Oh yes, of course") Hannah with such a "cute" project. I ignored these distractions. With every passing hour I grew more and more attached to my ants. A dollop of honey on the driveway lured a herd of them from the Bermuda Triangle of our lawn. Old Popsicle sticks worked well for the transfer into large mason jars. I stabbed holes in the top with needles, and sometimes you could see the little legs poking through. "Ew," Agnes said, "grody." Despite her fragile stomach, she helped me transplant the ants into their new homes. Occasionally we crushed them between our fingers, or smashed them with the Popsicle sticks, and then we would have a solemn ten seconds of silence for each little death. But for the most part, everything went smoothly.

It was in one of my ant-fueled reveries, wondering what made one ant happy and the next sluggish, that I discovered Custom Ant-farm Creation. I explained this to a boy from my class, a boy named Viktor who had ridden his bike all the way from the valley to see what we were doing.

"What does that mean?" he asked me, picking up a farm and shaking it like an etch-a-sketch.

"Don't do that, please," I said. "It agitates them."

"What does custom creation mean?"

"Well," I explained, delighted to find an interested patron, "let's say you don't want any old ant farm. Let's say you want one where the ants are happier than regular ants, like a sort of Ant Playground or something, or let's say you want one where the ants are super hard workers, three times as fast or something. You can place the order with me. Within a week I'll make your ant farm happy, or fast, or jumpy, or whatever."

Viktor seemed to like this idea. He looked at my sister, who sat beside me at the table fiddling with a pencil and staring up at him like he was made of gold. "What about horny ants," he said.

"Oh, Viktor," I laughed, "don't say that in front of Agnes."

Agnes blushed and Viktor smiled. Then he said to me, "It's not Victor. It's Viktor."

"That's what I said."

"No, you didn't. You say it wrong. I'm Vick-TOR, and you say it 'Vick-TER.'"

I looked confused. "What's the difference?"

"The difference," Agnes said, "is the TOR."

My knuckles itched.

"It's Russian," Viktor said. "I'm a direct descendant of the Tsar."

"What Tsar?" I asked.

"What, you stupid or something?" Viktor said.

Agnes giggled.

"You her older sister?" he asked her.

"She's two years younger than me, Vick-TOR."

He whistled. "Could have fooled me."

The thing was, I had always liked Viktor. I liked that in class he didn't speak a lot, and that some of the other kids seemed to find him annoying. They treated him sort of the same way they treated me, as if he had a cow's head sprouting from one shoulder. We were both skinny and pale, too. In the right light we looked translucent. I daydreamed about how our children would come out of our mansion squinting into the light, all wormy and bone-white, bitter and smart.

Agnes, of course, had pink cheeks and actual boobs. She had gotten her period a year before I'd had mine. This made her somewhat awkward in her own year, I'd noticed, but had also given her a sort of other-worldly appeal. It had been the disgrace of my life this last spring when, having discovered blood during a routine bathroom break at school, I'd had to ask my little sister for a maxi pad. She'd been friendly enough about it, but I could never shake the feeling that in the race to womanhood, I hadn't even made the B-squad.

Boys loved Agnes, of course. A few of them, some from her class, some older, skidded their bicycles to a stop on our driveway and glanced shyly into the garage. For the next several weeks, they treated our home like the parking lot in front of Jolly Cheezers, laughing loudly and exchanging jokes and ultimately pretending not to notice Agnes when any old idiot knew they were thinking of nothing else. Agnes poured soil into the plastic farms and ignored them just as efficiently. One of those short, bratty-looking boys said, without even trying to conceal his high voice, "They can't be sisters. Hannah's ugly as a horse," and then he blew such a huge snot-rocket onto the pavement that the other boys exclaimed, "Wicked!" Agnes's head snapped toward me and she said, "They suck. Nobody likes them." But I knew this was a lie. They were the most popular boys at school. The fact that they sought her out like so many heat-seeking missiles meant only one thing: she was the most popular girl. Over the summer, the shame, like the heat, only thickened.

After the first few weeks, the numbers of interested parties grew scarce. Uncle Hayward didn't return the lonely mothers' and housewives' flirtations, so they eventually retreated back into their expensive homes. The boys on their bikes still stopped by, but having less of a people-screen to hide behind, they grew skittish like lambs and stayed for shorter and shorter periods of time. Agnes and I still spent most of our days in the garage or on the driveway. I wore bruises into my knees and palms from foraging the pavement for more ants. There were now mason jars swarming with them. I had yet to find a queen.

Even though I protested, Uncle Hayward forced us to slow production. We could search for queens, he said, but we didn't need more ants. He also suggested we keep the ants in a shadier place. "They'll fry like bacon," he warned. I pinned up signs in the coolest corner of the garage. They read, in alphabetical order, "Eager Farms," "Happy Farms," "Hardworking Farms," "Super Farms," "Wonderful Farms." Hayward asked, "What's the difference? They're all the same."

I knew that was baloney. "Believe me," I told him. "Every ant has its own personality."

Hayward laughed and ruffled my hair. "Don't take yourself too seriously, kiddo."

It took all of my newfound benevolence to just grit my teeth and smile.

The good thing, at first, was that Viktor kept stopping by. One day, I showed him the Horny Ant Farm I had made (without, of course, Hayward's knowing). When he lifted it off of my workstation and peered through the plastic walls, he only said, "Nah. There's no humping."

I laughed, despite feeling hurt. How was I supposed to know there should be humping? I told him, "Take it anyway. It's a gift."

For the first time ever, he looked straight at me. "Wow, really? Thanks." He tucked the farm under his arm and asked, "Where's Agnes?"

I frowned. "Who cares?"

Viktor clucked his tongue and stared off into the distance. "I'm in love with her," he said dreamily.

"You're stupid," I hollered at him, much louder than necessary. "She's stupid and you're stupider."

Viktor frowned. "What's your prob? You jealous? Jealous that your sister's pretty? Jealous you're such a rat?"

Hayward heard the yelling and came over from the yard, where he had been sunning himself and listening to the radio.

"What's going on?" he asked.

"I was just leaving," Viktor said, and shoved the ant farm at me. I took it from him, about to cry. "I don't want your stupid farm. They aren't Horny Ants. They're Stupid Ants. Those are the only ants you can make, Hannah."

He cycled away.

Hayward said, "Horny ants?"

"He hates me," I wailed. Hayward sat down next to me and patted his knee. I perched there and wiped at my face. It was strange sitting on a grown man's knee. I hadn't sat on my own father's knee in years.

"He doesn't hate you," Hayward said. "He probably has a crush on you. That's how boys act."

I shook my head. "Viktor likes Agnes," I said. "All the boys do. He said," I started crying again, "he said I was a rat."

Hayward hugged me and kissed the back of my head. "Now, now. You don't believe that, do you? It's not true." His breath smelled of Altoids and cigarettes.

"He likes *her*," I said resolutely. Hayward let me go and I stood up. "He does. Just ask her."

Hayward looked troubled. "She's so young," he said.

"Not to him."

"Maybe I should say something." Hayward looked at me as though wanting my approval.

"Yes. Definitely. You should."

I hoped a boy-related conversation with Uncle Hayward would humiliate Agnes. At least a little bit.

Then Agnes appeared on her bike, looping slowly around the driveway. "What's wrong?" she called.

"Nothing," I said.

"Let's look for a queen." She dismounted and let the bike crash to the pavement.

I wiped at my face and said okay. Even Hayward helped. I knelt at a small hole in the yard from where I had seen some ants emerge, and I waited. "There's a queen down there," I whispered. I was going to find her and capture her and make an ant-farm immortal. Viktor would read about me in the papers, when I had become a famous entomologist, and he would regret his terrible behavior. He would call me up and I would laugh. Then I would tell him – but right then I saw a long, strange, winged ant. It moved sluggishly from the small hole and into the light. My heart thudded. I put my hand gingerly over it. "I've got one!" I screamed. "I've got a queen!"

Agnes was impressed. "That's so cool," she said, after we had transferred it to a farm. I was beaming. Uncle Hayward patted me on the back.

"See?" he said. "Life's not so bad."

I shrugged. But right then, life did feel pretty great.

Later that night, the phone rang during dinner. Dad hated it when the phone rang. "For the love of Christopher," he said, standing, "can't a man enjoy his dinner without being interrupted?"

"You could turn the ringer off," Mom suggested. She always suggested this.

"It could be Elias." This was always Dad's reply. Elias was Dad's boss.

Moments later, Dad returned from the den. "That was some snotty-sounding kid for Agnes. A Victor or something?"

"Viktor, Dad," Agnes corrected.

"Aren't you, what, ten years old?" Dad said. "What's with the opposite-sex phone calls?"

Agnes looked embarrassed. "I dunno. He's never called before." She saw me glowering at her and said over a forkful of peas, "What, Hannah? I think he's stupid."

"Ha," I said. "So do I. Too bad he loves you."

Mom said, "Is this the little Russian boy from your class, Hannah? I find the Russians so fascinating."

"He's not a Russian, Mom. He's a liar."

"Hannah," she scolded, "it's not polite to disallow someone their cultural heritage."

The whole time, Hayward sat there regarding Agnes with his face all scrunched up. His concern gathered when Dad handed her an index card complete with Viktor's misspelled name and telephone number.

"Is this such a good idea?" Hayward asked the table. "She's a ten-year-old girl. Perhaps it's not such a good idea. If this boy is pursuing her, after all."

I loved Hayward for saying this.

"Oh please, Hayward," Dad boomed, "what sort of twelve-year-old boy could even recognize his dick in a line-up?"

Mom gasped. "Brett, please!" Then she peered closer at the index card. "Oh!" she gasped delightedly. "That's a downtown number. You should call him, Agnes, and invite him over tomorrow. The poor thing doesn't breathe a drop of fresh air in that neighborhood."

Hayward put his hands over his face. I could tell he was on my side.

Later that night, while Dad snored in front of the television and Mom went to take one of her lengthy peach-smelling baths, I went to the garage to read comics with my penlight on the old sofa Hayward had stored in one corner. I had just been getting to a great scene where Antzilla crushes all those who have ever tried to smash her, when light from the kitchen fell in a yellow rectangle across the hood of Dad's car. Hayward and Agnes entered, Hayward shutting the door softly behind them. I catapulted over the back of the couch with my comic book, and then sat cross-legged against the couch's moldy spine. I shut off my penlight. For some reason, Hayward did not switch on the overhead lamp.

On the way to the couch, they bumped into things. Agnes said, "I'm sorta afraid of the dark."

Uncle Hayward replied in no more than a whisper, "Don't worry, we're almost there." They sat down. I could smell the rising dust.

At first, I was impressed with what Hayward was saying. He told Agnes, "It's not right, that boy with you. It's just not."

"Cause he's in Hannah's class?"

"Well, that, and that he wants to take advantage of you."

I imagined that Agnes was, per usual, confused by Hayward's remarks.

"Look," Hayward said, "some boys are nice boys. Some are mean. That Viktor. He's a bad seed. He does not want to be nice to you, do you see? I think he wants to be mean to you."

"But Hannah likes him," Agnes said. After a moment's pause, she suggested, "Maybe she should date him."

"Sure, sure. Hannah should date him. But you're too lovely for those boys." I heard, then, the sound of one body snuggling closer to the other. Then Hayward grunted as if he were lifting something. My eyes slowly adjusted to the dark. It took me a moment to figure out that Agnes was now seated squarely on Hayward's lap, both of them facing away from me.

In the dark, her head appeared to be growing from out of his right shoulder.

"I want to be nice to you," he said.

"You're always nice, Uncle Hayward."

"Do you want me to be nice to you?"

"Well, sure." Agnes's voice sounded tighter now, almost annoyed. Then she said, as though eager for a subject change, "Isn't it cool that Hannah found a queen?"

Hayward's voice was muffled, in her hair or something. "That wasn't a queen. I didn't want to tell her, the poor thing, but that was just a young male ant. You need to dig up a queen, you know. They look almost the same, I guess, but you're not going to find some queen just randomly roaming around."

"Oh," Agnes said. "Sucky."

"Our little secret, though, right?" Hayward whispered this. I could hear his hands groping.

The tips of my ears flushed hot. I thought about the winged ant, something that looks special, but really is not. I bit my lip to keep from bawling. I wanted to believe that Hayward was wrong, but some dark part of me knew that he was right.

"You're the most beautiful girl," Hayward said, and began kissing the back of her neck. It was not the same way he had kissed the back of my head. It was not with dry, unparted lips. It was puckered and smacking, like when Mom pressed a wet sponge onto a plate.

"That tickles," Agnes said. I could see that she was squirming.

"Just be quiet for a moment. Let me be nice to you." He shuffled around on the couch again. "The most beautiful little girl. The most precious thing."

I hated him so much. *The most beautiful little girl. The most precious thing.* I groped around for something, anything, to hurt him with, and what I came up with was one of my mason jars filled with about three-hundred ants. I unscrewed the jar. The lid made a rasping sound, the air escaping in one soft sigh, smelling sour like pee. Agnes said, "What was that?" but Uncle Hayward panted loudly in her ear, "I should stop. I should really stop," and she said, sounding bored, "This is sorta weird. I want to go in now, Uncle Hayward." I squatted behind them and turned over the jar right above the dark heavy line of his shoulders. The next second they were up on their feet, and he was screaming. The garage flooded with light. Dad stood at the top of the stairs, gaping. When my eyes adjusted, I saw Agnes standing there calmly, blinking, with part of her t-shirt pushed over the top of her right boob. Hayward was shaking himself and tearing off his shirt and begging for help.

"What's going on here?" Dad roared.

"Hayward was being nice to me," Agnes said, not without disgust. Ants glided from the open mason jar onto my fingers and up my arm. Dad stared, silent. Hayward wept and squirmed. Mom materialized and the sounds grew loud and sharp. Somehow Agnes and I were ushered inside. We sat on the floor of my bedroom together and said nothing. She picked an ant out of my hair and asked if I wanted to play cards. I said okay.

That was the last time we ever saw Hayward. The next day, while Mom continued to panic and make doctor's appointment after doctor's appointment for Agnes, Dad tossed out all of our ant farms. I asked if I could keep even one, the one with the winged ant, and he said "No." Agnes tried to come to my defense. "But the ants were what saved me," she said. But even her perfect charm failed. Dad would have none of it.

Agnes, of course, was fine. "He only kissed my neck and touched my boob," Agnes said. I said to her, and also to Mom, "He kissed me, too." Mom didn't seem too worried about me. She wrote a letter to Oprah, describing how her brother had molested her littlest daughter without her even realizing it. "And under my own roof, Oprah!" One of Oprah's representatives called a couple of weeks later and asked if they'd come on a special show, "Blind Mothers, Molested Daughters." Mom was ecstatic. I asked if I was going to be on the show, too. She said no.

Dad and I flew to Chicago with them, anyway. We watched the show from a fancy hotel. Dad seemed embarrassed, seeing them on-screen. Mom was so excited that she couldn't stop grinning, even when Agnes told Oprah, "Then he touched my boob and kissed my neck."

Dad said, "Your mother looks psychotic."

When they came back, we all went for a walk on the lake. Mom and Dad sat on a park bench and watched us from afar.

"Did you see the show?" Agnes asked. She was sullen.

"Yeah."

"Did you hear what I said about you?"

I shook my head.

"Maybe they cut it. I told them you saved me. You and the ants."

"Really?"

"Yeah."

We walked along silently, kicking at stones. "I guess it must kind of suck for you," I said.

"Nah. One of the girls on the show I felt so sorry for. Some dude stuck his wiener in her!"

"Ick," I said. We kind of laughed.

"I can't believe they cut that," she said, "what I said about you."

I didn't exactly trust her, but it made me kinder toward her. Even if she hadn't told Oprah that I was her hero, she had at least admitted it to me. I would always have one-up on her for that.

We stood at the water's edge and let it lick the tips of our sandals. "This water smells like bird poop," I said.

"I wish I could lop these things off and toss them into the waves." She was looking down at her breasts.

I didn't say anything. I couldn't tell if this was all a performance or not.

We went back to the hotel and ordered cokes and chicken-strips and French fries with extra ketchup through room service. When we had successfully pigged-out, Agnes and I put on our pajamas and brushed our teeth. Mom and Dad went to the bar downstairs, saying they'd be back soon. "Don't let anyone in here," Mom warned. The heavy door locked squarely behind them.

Alone, we flipped through all of the channels that we weren't supposed to watch. In the scratchy grayness of one station, the screen swarming with herds of black ants, we could hear moans, and we could see a thigh here, a breast there, slightly unfamiliar game pieces of shuddering bodies.

"Shut it off," Agnes said.

I did.

I wouldn't mind taking orders from her sometimes. If I could be her hero, then that meant she was salvageable. It wasn't too hard to accept surrender then. But there were times, following, when out of either anger or pity I almost admitted, *Hey, I saved you for all the wrong reasons.*

∨∨∨∨∨∨∨∨∨∨∨∨∨∨∨∨∨∨∨∨∨∨∨∨∨∨∨∨

NEIGHBORHOOD

∧∧∧∧∧∧∧∧∧∧∧∧∧∧∧∧∧∧∧∧∧∧∧∧∧∧∧∧

The Johnsons started it all with the fountain, a marble statue of an embracing fish and woman. It was nearly two stories tall. When I first saw it I regretted living alone. We're talking erotic. The paperboy paled when he pedaled by on his ten-speed. I could hear him swallow from my breakfast nook. The fish shared his frightened expression, the wide-eyed terror of someone trapped. The woman gripped the fish relentlessly, her lips parted in lust. Her manhole-sized nipples bore down on us like great eyeballs. It was a challenge. A velvet glove cast at our feet. We turned critical eyes onto our own yards.

The Heybeckers responded grandly, carrying out coils of Christmas lights and draping them around their two small children. The children lived outdoors from this moment on, playing during the day and glowing sleepily from lawn chairs at night. They were polite, winsome children who waved at my car as I drove to and from work. It was a daily joy to watch Mrs. Heybecker pad onto the parapet with fresh pizza or a cookie and call out her children's monikers. "Piggy! Lion! Are you alright my little sweetums, my little works of art?" They ran to her eagerly, careful not to trip over the wires, and lifted their hungry faces up to her like baby birds. On rainy days the children hunkered on the stoop, frowning, their sharp sturdy knees tucked under their chins. When the sun came out they soared slowly into the yard with their arms outstretched like airplanes. Lights glittered around them at all times so that in the dark they resembled miniature mountain towns, like two Quitos, two Denvers. They never had to go to school again, or read another book. They became wild and dirty and introspective.

The Bjorns, childless, but clearly inspired by the glitter of the young children three houses removed, dragged several television sets of various sizes into their garden beds. They sat tilted and strange in the dirt, like uncovered treasures. There were perhaps two dozen sets in all, their wires cleverly hidden in the earth, each issuing a distinct channel: a telenovela here, a newscast there, a reality show to the left of the apple tree, below the bougainvillea an infomercial for fireproof pants. During the day the voices of the televisions' residents clamored and chattered competitively, which was exhausting at first, but if you stood there long enough they began to sound like a pleasant primordial chorus – like crickets in a field or frogs in a pond. Around eight o'clock every evening Mr. Bjorn wandered through the yard in his Batman pajamas, taking up the remote controls from the top of each set and muting them one by one so that the squares of light fell silent, the only noise then the static and hum of their electricity. Months passed and August came. Weeds, oregano and mint sprouted alongside the glowing bellies of the sets and wrapped around them so that during the newscasts the weatherman appeared to be choked by Amazonian vines. The effect was a pleasant one. We neighbors sometimes gathered before the Bjorn yard to gaze yearningly at the televisions, hoping to glean some knowledge of the world at large.

The Bjorn lawn was certainly the most traditional on the street and was eventually photographed for *Better Homes and Gardens*. I snuck into the background of one of these photographs. If you use a magnifying glass, you can see me clearly. There I am, resting against someone's blue Ford, the woman with the brown curly hair and the scarred forehead and the t-shirt that reads, "Livin' Large in the Lilac City." I've since framed this magazine clipping and hung it over the air purifier in my living room. It's wonderful to feel part of something so special.

And it was special. We neighbors had not meant to unify. We had meant to compete. But from the splendor of our yards camaraderie bloomed. This happens when people find a common interest. It doesn't matter the subject. It could be a role-playing game or a TV actress or a football team. We bonded over our interest and we alienated outsiders with it. That is the meaning of camaraderie.

Not surprisingly, our neighborhood became the envy of the town. People from other neighborhoods voyaged south and drove slowly down our street, their jaws dropping in awe. All of the houses boasted ambitious lawns: the Smees with their disco gazebo, the Hos with their confetti sprinklers, the Polanskis with their garden of hair, and me with The Forest. Initially, I was worried about my lack of originality, but then I decided I would find originality in the formulaic. I was, I say humbly, successful.

I started with birdbaths and birdfeeders. Sparrow and quail and robins arrived and twittered prettily, but the neighbors were understandably not impressed. I set out some sunflower seeds and drew in squirrels and chipmunks. I hung some red water feeders for hummingbirds. The children across the street glittered in their Christmas lights and stared. I put a salt lick on my stoop and two deer wandered down from the forest. They had delicate spindly legs and hesitant bobbing heads. I watched them the first morning through my kitchen window and held my breath, drinking in their loveliness.

The second morning I pointed a dart gun through a hole in the screen and shot them full of tranquilizers.

When they woke up they tugged wildly against their fetters and reared with frightened white eyes. I clucked at them and tried to pet their noses and offered them carrots like you would a horse, but this only aggravated them. Their white tails lifted and fell like flashes of lightning. Their nostrils flared so wildly that I feared they might tear.

I awoke the third morning to find a crowd gathered on my porch, admiring my work. The deer were stomping, panicking. Mr. Smythe playfully poked at them with a golf club. I stood barefoot in the yard with my coffee mug and my cucumber mask melting on my face. The deer, surrounded by my neighbors, were more frenetic than ever.

This all reminded me of a childhood visit to Disneyland. I had been standing for nearly an hour in a long line on a street corner to see Bambi, who was signing autograph books and walking on his hind legs, and when it was finally my turn Goofy appeared and told me that Bambi needed a cigarette break. I waited patiently while Bambi smoked in the dim alley of a fish and chips restaurant. I was just able to see his long profile, the fabric hoof ritually lifting the cigarette to his snout. Pigeons were everywhere, pecking and crapping, and he kicked at one that wandered too close. Eventually he dropped the butt and stepped on it with his hoof, and returned to me with an audible sigh. "Okay, kid," he said, collecting himself, and his big hairy fingers reached out from the hoof, gripping a pen and reeking of cloves. I stammered for something to say and failed. Bambi patted my head in a friendly way and then turned dismissively to the boy behind me.

"Bambi's killing himself," my dad commented blandly as we walked away. "He may as well have died in the fire." My heart shattered – as much pained by my father's angry judgment of my favorite cartoon character as I was hurt by Bambi's perverse theme-park portrayal. "Don't ever smoke, sweetie," dad added. With those words Disneyland was dead to me. I went back to the hotel and wept as dark descended and wouldn't even surface when Dad promised jalapeño poppers for dinner.

And now these deer, these beautiful thriving creatures, trapped in my faux-natural yard. Everyone was agreeing that I should be given the blue ribbon. As the deer buckled and snorted against their ropes, I worried aloud that they might die of fright.

Mr. Johnson shook his head and said admiringly, "'Art washes away from the soul the dust of everyday life.' Some artist guy said that, I don't remember who."

Mrs. Smee, weeping with joy as she tried vainly to pet the deer's head, added, "Art brings us joy but does not hide from us sorrow."

The children across the street, cocooned in their Christmas lights, hollered from the Heybecker yard, "Out of death comes rebirth!"

The ribbon ceremony was the next day. I had already cleared off a place near my air purifier for the display. But later that evening I was alone with my frightened deer, watching their sorrowful bowed heads. At midnight, while the glittering children snored peacefully from their lawn chairs across the street, and while the television sets blazed like angry watchful gods from the corner lot, I tiptoed outside and labored to untie the ropes that cut into the deer's necks. Finally the knots fell free. With a fury that seemed to break the numbness of my daily life, the deer crashed into the trees behind my house and disappeared, swallowed up by a wilderness both terrifying and good.

The next morning my house was passed over with hardly a glance. Sans the captive deer it was a pedestrian yard, unremarkable. Coincidentally, this was the same morning that the marble baby materialized in the Johnsons' fountain. It had the body of a fish and the head of a man. It was adorable.

The blue ribbon, we agreed unanimously, would go to them.

THE TYLENOL CHEERLEADER

∧∧∧∧∧∧∧∧∧∧∧∧∧∧∧∧∧∧∧∧∧∧∧∧∧∧∧∧

1. Press Release

To cut down on advertising costs while maintaining consumer affection, McNeil-PPC, Inc., the makers of Tylenol®, announce the new drug Periphirol. Combined with a regular dose of extra-strength acetamino-phen, Periphirol releases a light hallucinogenic that, upon blood-stream dissolution, displays in the consumer's subconscious the image of Alice, the Tylenol Cheerleader.

Alice is the champion for those suffering from minor-to-severe headaches, backaches and menstrual cramps. Approximately fifteen to twenty minutes post-consumption, Alice appears within the customer's field of vision. At the end of her brief and unassuming dance routine, Alice grins winningly and arcs her red-and-yellow Tylenol pompoms over her head. The pathway of this arc forms a rainbow wherein reads the words, *Tylenol Rocks!* The customer may then choose to ignore Alice, or discuss politics with her, or merely enjoy her long legs and impressive gymnastic capabilities. Within four to six hours, she disappears as the effectiveness of the acetaminophen fades.

While the FDA was initially concerned about Periphirol, tests on monkeys and rats proved the drug to be no more harmful than television commercials and billboards. The only setback was when Andrew, also known as Monkey #82, developed what seemed to be an unnatural fond-ness for Alice, eventually rendering his glass cage uninhabitable, at least until the janitor cleaned it out with Windex. Andrew's affections, as the FDA has pointed out, can be attributed to the charming Hollywood hybrid of Alice's blonde beauty. "And," one FDA representative added, "to the awe-some dance moves of a very young and very bouncy Paula Abdul," as Alice's athleticism was computer generated to match those of the star's Laker Girls days. That being said, the FDA assures the public that the chance of human males responding in a similar fashion to Monkey #82 is highly unlikely. As another FDA rep said, "Her sweater's unrevealing."

Children love Alice's large blue eyes, almond-shaped to match those of Disney characters. Women appreciate Alice's excellent taste and accepting smile, as well as her ability to discuss Oprah while performing high-kicks. Men enjoy Alice's ability to kick back a beer and watch sports. Indeed, Alice has something for everyone. She's been especially programmed to be un-dismissible.

Periphirol-laced Tylenol® hits Wal-Mart shelves early next week. A friendlier, less annoying method of advertisement, Periphirol is likely to eradicate television commercials, magazine ads and billboards. It gives consumers a choice: you can see the ad if you want to, or you can just allow it to roam around in your subconscious mind, entirely unnoticed.

"I'd take that any day," Duluth resident Charles Pinkley says. "Commercials blow. Alice is way better. I'm going to buy a six-pack and just lounge around with her all weekend."

For his input, Mr. Pinkley was given a year's supply of Tylenol®.

2. *Joan Worthington*

I have this problem when I'm in a public bathroom. I have to pick up every scrap of toilet paper or paper towel and throw them away. Even the wet, soiled ones. When someone's in the bathroom with me, the tips of my fingers itch. I'll *try* not to clean. I'll wait for a couple of minutes for the woman to enter a stall or exit altogether and sometimes she won't, and then I just swallow my pride and bend and retrieve.

Last week, a girl with pink eyelashes and green hair said to me, "Whoa. What are you doing?"

"Cleaning up," I said. I casually pushed a wet paper towel into the trash bin. It was smeared with something mysterious and brown. I had found it mashed into a corner of the restaurant's bathroom stall.

"Freaky," the girl said, but she sounded bored. Then she turned back to the mirror to apply more mascara.

I left the bathroom embarrassed but gnawingly satisfied that the floor was litter-free. I was so satisfied that I went next door, into a gas station, to ask if I could use their restroom. I was worried that it would continue forever, that I would keep collecting and tossing until I was so thin from hunger and sleeplessness that I, too, would become a piece of paper on the floor. But it only continued for five more public bathrooms, and then I felt okay.

When I got home, I dumped Clorox on the kitchen floor. I wanted to talk to Delia, the Clorox Housewife. I inhaled hard and leaned against the wall. She appeared in front of me, her teeth glittering like pearls, her apron awash with fluorescent dots.

"Delia," I told her, putting my hands together in supplication. "I need help." I felt a horrible urge to sob. "I'm so lonely."

Delia laughed, shaking her rag. "You're making the world more beautiful. Just like me, don't you see? You're one of my angels. One of my sweet dears."

I closed my eyes and inhaled. Delia twirled about, singing, wiping things down.

3. Alice, The Tylenol Cheerleader

Don't look so sour, Chuck. Be happy. Smiling is the best way to conquer pain. Laughter is the best medicine.

Tylenol Rocks!

When my knee starts to ache, either from surgery or from arthritis or from a nasty bump on the coffee table, I take a Tylenol, and it works fast. It works fast so that I can keep kicking…cartwheeling…leaping…my way to victory.

Tylenol Rocks!

Don't be so glum, Chuck. Laughter is the best medicine. And so is Tylenol. Tylenol works fast so that you can, too.

When I have a headache, I can't stop for pain. I have to work at the office, or babysit my grandchildren, or amp up the student section of the bleachers. When Boss Edgar is yelling, Finish this brief!, or tiny Tina's pleading, Read *Munster Land* again!, or the crowd is just going ballistic, my headache threatens to destroy all that is good in the world. But ten minutes after I pop a Tylenol, I feel great again. I can write, read, cheer, and appreciate the good things that my super-swell life has to offer.

Tylenol Rocks!

So let's go out to the garage. Open the car door. Turn the key. Reverse. Take a right here, onto 1st Avenue. Now, take a left. While at this stop sign, watch me do a triple pike into a split. Now press the gas. Okay. Not that fast. We'll get there, I promise. There's no reason to put your – I mean our – lives in danger. The Sav-and-Pay is just ahead. Everything you need in the world is only a block away.

vvvvvvvvvvvvvvvvvvvvvvvvv

SUNSHINE AND
THE PREDATOR

∧∧∧∧∧∧∧∧∧∧∧∧∧∧∧∧∧∧∧∧∧∧∧∧∧

Dad said, If you're bored, be like the Blue Collar Kids. Get a frigging job.

A week later, I interviewed with Harold Gibbons, General Manager of Lilac City Theme Parks. He was a burly man. His heavy pink face shone with sweat. His office was sweltering and smelled vaguely like melted cheese.

"How old?" he asked me.

"I just turned fourteen."

"What grade?"

"Freshman. Sophomore in the fall."

"You some kind of genius or something?"

"No," I said. "I just skipped a grade."

"Eh. No wonder you're so thin."

He sucked on his large gums and motioned for me to follow. The park was sandblasted with sun and very vacant. We walked down a road painted to look like yellow bricks and then down a smaller pathway painted to look like dirt.

"Nice paint," I said. "It looks really real."

"Eh."

"Did you paint this?" I asked. Gibbons laughed.

"Are you kidding?" He loosened the brown tie at his neck and shook his head. Dad had told me, *Keep your mouth shut. Just smile.* My cheeks wobbled. Gibbons ignored me.

The fake dirt pathway led to a big mechanical apparatus. Lights and buzzers were going off and really loud speakers played Metallica. The ride rotated around a large red column painted with screaming faces. On the floor, secured by screws the size of my head, were seats that looked like the booths in a pizza joint, except these booths were missing a table and had seatbelts.

"The Rock 'N' Roller," Gibbons said. "It's not one of our most exciting rides, but it pulls in a decent amount of clients."

"Wow," I yelled over the music, "it's really, really neat!"

"This machine is not a toy." Gibbons glanced at me, annoyed. "It's dangerous. I once found a raccoon pulverized between the rotating floor and the bars underneath. And raccoons, you know, are bigger than some babies."

I nodded, genuinely afraid. "Do people take babies on these rides?"

Gibbons turned away from me and hollered, "Joan! Come here. I want you to meet Miss Sunshine."

A girl staring at us from the ticket console licked her lips and approached. She was wearing jean shorts and a bikini top. I recognized her from gym class. We were usually the last selections for team lineups.

"Hi Joan," I said.

"Oh," she blinked. "It's you. Yeah, hey. What's up."

"Great. You two know one another." Gibbons glanced at his watch and burped. "Listen, Erin here is going to be our new ride operator."

"Alright." Joan shrugged. "Whatever."

"Joan handles the tickets. Now she won't have to do both."

"Yeah." Joan rolled her eyes and snorted. "I *really* need the help. It's *so* fricking busy."

"Great. I'll let you two catch up then." To me Gibbons said, "Come and see me when you're finished here." When he hit the pathway, he turned around to shout at Joan, "And put on some clothes, young lady!"

Once he was out of earshot, I told Joan, "He's really nice."

"Sure." She snapped a shoulder strap on her bikini. "A real peach."

"How long have you known him?"

"Ha," she said. "Just my whole life."

"I don't – "

"He's my uncle, nitwit." Joan's eyes crawled over me. "What was your last name again? Sunshine?"

"Oh no," I laughed. "No, that was his name for me, not my real name. I'm Erin. Erin Crubbsfeld."

"Your Dad's on those commercials, right? Crubbsfeld Developers or whatever?" When I nodded, she whistled all low and exaggerated. "That's muy, muy impressive."

"Muy?"

"It's Spanish for very."

"Oh," I said, trying to sound casual. I stood there like I was made of coat hangers. "That's really cool."

"Anyway, Sunshine," Joan said, "this job's a cakewalk. Kids get stoned, give tickets, get on, get off. No problem. Sometimes you can get free joints."

"Joints?" I winced at the fear in my voice and wished that I had kept my mouth shut, but Joan didn't seem to notice. She just rambled on, scratching at her lip with a blood-red fingernail.

"This ride is like sitting in a car. People always bitch about it. But there's never puke. That's one major plus. Still, there's mopping at the end of the night. Dirt from people's shoes and stuff." She brightened here, "And since you're the new girl, the mopping is your job."

This didn't exactly seem fair, but Dad was always mentioning hierarchies, and so I guessed I'd be what he'd describe as The-Low-Girl-On-The-Totem-Pole. Maybe it would be a good thing. One of Dad's favorite mantras was, *Humiliation Begets Dignity.*

"Well I suppose," I said, growing uncomfortably sweaty in my interview clothes, "I should go and talk to your uncle about times and stuff. You know, work-related stuff."

"Yeah," she nodded. "I guess."

My face had grown tomato red. I waved and walked quickly away.

"Adios, Sunshine!" Joan hollered over the Metallica.

Dad laughed when I told him I got the Job. *Gibbons must have liked your honest face.*

When I arrived for the first day of work, a guy dressed in a clown suit was sitting with Joan in one of the Rock 'N' Roller booths, his white hand creeping up her thigh. His oversized goods – ultra-large plastic glasses and bright balloons twisted into animal shapes – bloomed like weird tropical flowers from the booth behind them. He smiled at me through his painted-on frown. He looked like the reason people are afraid of clowns.

"Hello," I said, waving.

Joan saw me, leaned into the clown and whispered something through his fuzzy red wig. They bent away from one another, laughing. He slapped her thigh gently. I gulped.

"When should I…get started?"

Joan rolled her eyes.

"Just hang out, Sunshine. No one shows up until sundown anyway."

"Hang out?" I asked.

The rotating floor wasn't rotating, the heavy metal wasn't blaring.

"Yeah," she said, "just chill out."

The clown wouldn't stop grinning at me through his big, painted frown. I shuddered.

"This is Eli!" Joan shouted. "He's a real clown." They started laughing again.

I didn't want to stand there like a ghoul, ogling them, so I went and sat by myself on the stairs, hugging my legs. The sun toasted my arms. I put my head down on the warmth and dozed off.

Then a big hand was shaking me awake.

"Hey Princess!" Gibbons roared. "You're neglecting this machine. Do you know what happens when you neglect this machine? Clients die! Babies die!"

Raccoons die. I rose to my feet sputtering, "Oh – I'm – sorry, I…"

I looked to Joan for help. She lolled in a booth, alone now, reading a thick romance novel.

"Aw, leave her alone," Joan said, without looking up from her book. "I told her to just hang out. There's no reason to start blasting music before people even get here, Uncle Harold."

Gibbons pivoted his big blotchy body toward her. "You want to keep your job, right?"

Joan shut her mouth. She pretended to be reading.

"Answer me."

"Yes, Uncle Harold." She put the book down between her knees and sulked.

Then, to me, he said, "She gives you any trouble, you come and talk to me, alright?"

"Yes sir," I nodded. "I will right away, sir."

He straightened, putting his hands on his hips, gazing at me as if confused. He shifted to Joan and said, "Behave, young lady." And then he was gone.

"Aw," she said, coming over and sitting beside me on the stairs, "he's a pain in the butt. Muy, muy annoying."

I bit my lip and tried not to cry. She frowned.

"What's the matter?" she asked.

"I feel awful," I blubbered, "I don't want to get fired."

"You're not going to get fired," Joan laughed. Her blonde hair caught the sun and tossed it back. "You know what you have to do around here to get fired?"

I shook my head.

"Kill someone."

I didn't find it very funny, but I smiled and relaxed. My acrobatic stomach stopped its somersaulting.

The rest of the day went by fairly smoothly. Joan put me in charge of the CDs, which she said she only did for coworkers she could tolerate.

"It always has to be rock and roll," she instructed. "Songs about murder and sodomy and date rape. You'll either be sick of it or love it by the time school starts next fall."

I didn't ask what sodomy meant.

There weren't very many customers. Joan was right: it didn't get busy until sundown, and even then we hardly had more than five people on the ride at once. While The Dragon's Breath and The Tilt and Twirl elicited nervous laughter and girlish screams from its patrons, The Rock 'N' Roller gleaned only the occasional bored smile. Joan put me in charge of both the levers and the tickets. She went behind the ride to sit cross-legged on pavement that had been painted green to look like grass. She smoked cigarette after cigarette, returning with a dazed, at-peace expression and the smell of tobacco haloing her head. I didn't mind what she did as long as she was nice to me.

At 6PM, three pretty girls from our class came through the line.

"Justin is *so* lame for bringing us here," Alison said. They hadn't seen me yet, and I wished the light hanging over the ticket booth weren't quite so glaring.

"At least we get cotton candy. I frickin' *love* cotton candy," said another girl, Carlissa.

The last girl, one whose name I didn't know but whose face I recognized from the hallways, said, "Why dontcha marry it then?"

"Dude, that joke is *so* grandma," Alison said.

They stood at the stairs with their hands in the back pockets of their jeans. Their smooth hair was like freshly combed silk. They wore purses that swung on thin bands from their wrists. Petite and pretty and precious, these girls were like porcelain miniatures. In clothes that were too baggy and too short for my tall skinny frame, I loomed gangly and awkward like a scarecrow.

"Hi girls," I said when they filed up to me. "Tickets, please."

"Oh, hey," Alison said, "how's it going, Erin?"

"Ooh," Carlissa gushed. "You've got a Swissoma."

"Yeah." I looked down at my watch and touched it like I'd never seen it before. "My dad gave it to me."

"I've been asking for one for months," Carlissa continued, grabbing my wrist and twisting it toward her face for a better look.

While being examined, I smiled at Alison. She raised her eyebrows at me in response and then checked her fingernail polish. We played together when we were girls. Our parents lived in the same neighborhood on the South Hill. I wondered, standing there and waiting for Carlissa to release my wrist, if Alison shared any of my memories.

Joan materialized at my side, asking, "What time is it, anyway, Sunshine?" but then she saw the three girls and tensed. Carlissa let go of me.

"That's weird," the nameless girl said. "You work here, too?"

"Hey, Joan," Carlissa said, "let us on for free, wouldja? These tickets are a rip-off."

At my side, Joan's usually cool demeanor crumbled. She waved them through. The girls slid into a booth.

"What're the chances," I heard the nameless girl say to Alison and Carlissa, "that the class prude and the class slut would work here together?"

Alison turned and saw me watching. She buckled her seatbelt and said, half-smiling, "Hush, you twit. Everyone can hear you."

I started the ride. Screaming lyrics and guitars drowned out their laughter.

When it was time to shut down, I went out back and found Joan pacing slowly back and forth. She wore her empty pack of cigarettes like a paper tiara on top of her head.

"I'm not going back to school this fall," she said, walking and spinning on her invisible tightrope.

"Why not?" I asked. I was shocked. I had pictured us cruising around the halls together, stopping at our lockers to laugh at teachers and gossip about boys.

"School's not for me," she said. "It sucks there. Besides, Eli's eighteen and he's starting at Gonzaga in September. He says there's a whole rat race out there that he's made for. And he can be the breadwinner, you know? That's muy perfect with me."

I leaned against the back of the Rock 'N' Roller, next to an ugly thread of cords that twisted like intestines from the machine's gut.

"I think this job is pretty neat," I said casually, hoping to keep the conversation light. "I had fun working with you today."

Joan stopped pacing the tightrope and tilted her chin so that the empty cigarette pack swooped to the ground.

"Do you think those girls are pretty?" she asked.

"Alison and them?"

She nodded.

"Yeah, I do."

She looked disappointed.

I added quickly, "I used to be good friends with Alison, when we were little."

Joan ignored this.

"What about me. Do you think I'm pretty?"

"I think you're the prettiest girl I've ever seen," I said. "Way prettier than any of them."

And I really believed it. Especially when she smiled as she did then, and the dimples appeared next to her mouth like tiny pools of light. Her hair was supremely blonde, the sort of albino-blonde usually reserved for small children, and her eyes were wide and almost crossed, giving her a sort of candid innocence. She slouched like an older woman, comfortable with the body she was given, and although you could see that she was not particularly coordinated, there was a sort of curvy grace to her that the other girls lacked.

"It'd be neat to look like you," I said.

I supposed the word I was groping for was sexy, but even if I had thought of it, I would never have uttered it aloud.

"Aw, you don't mean that," Joan said.

I remained silent because I knew that she knew that I meant it. I meant it very much.

Joan smiled and seemed to forget her bad mood.

"Well," she said, "let's close shop. I'm muy famished." She set about, humming. With her back turned, I quickly retrieved the abandoned cigarette pack and placed it in the garbage can.

Dad called me into his office one night in July. *Andrew Gunderson told me about your trashy co-worker. Watch that she doesn't rub off on you.*

Andrew Gunderson was Eli Gunderson's father. He was also Dad's attorney.

I ignored what he said. Joan was one of the only girls my age that wanted to talk to me. It didn't bother me that she called me Sunshine, or that she left me alone, sometimes for hours, to eat cotton candy with Eli on the green pavement behind The Rock 'N' Roller. I was happy that I felt comfortable around her, and I admired that she wasn't such a Daddy's girl.

I told her this once and she said, "Well, it's easy when Daddy's dead."

I supposed that was why she lived downtown with Gibbons and his frail wife. I felt wretched for bringing it up. When I apologized, Joan said, "No prob," which made me like her even more.

The job, itself, was inconsistent. Whole nights would pass with maybe three customers. Other nights I would be there late, mopping up dirt and spilled soda, while Joan skipped down the fake dirt and out to freedom. The most exciting time was when some boy dropped his baseball cap. He unbuckled his seatbelt mid-ride and crawled over to the edge of the rotating floor to retrieve it. I roared "Hold on!" at him with a voice louder than I had ever used in my entire life, and then slowed the floor to a stop. "You could get your fingers caught," I scolded. "This floor is not a toy." The boy gaped at me. His lower lip trembled. It was better to have a frightened boy than a dead one. Joan was impressed and relayed the event to Gibbons. He gave me my first ever ten-cent raise.

Even Dad was proud. *Ten cents doesn't seem like much, but it all adds up.*

The best days were the days when Eli didn't show up, when I didn't have to slink away and leave the two of them alone. On those days, Joan and I would shut down The Rock 'N' Roller early and in the moonlight pet the goats and llamas and horses in the Livery Stables, where all the workers dressed like they were from the nineteenth century and said things like, "Spectacular night for a stroll, ain't it ma'am?"

Joan would make faces at them and try to draw them out of character. Her favorite trick was pointing at the animals whenever they pooped. Once she even pointed at a poop and said, "Hey! That looks like your face, Sunshine!" which actually made a couple of the workers snigger. When she saw my expression, she punched me on the arm. "Hey, I'm *kidding*. Geesh. It doesn't look like you at all." She paused to pinch her chin, regarding it carefully. "Actually, it looks like Eli." And then I was free to laugh along with her.

One night I accompanied the two of them, per Eli's suggestion, to get some cokes. Joan withdrew from me, as she always did when he appeared. Whenever I tried to be in step with her, she sped up, or slowed down, or moved to his opposite side so that he would be in between us. I walked a few paces behind them instead. Eli laughed.

"Geesh, Joan," he said. "Is this how you treat your friends?"

Joan threw me an over-the-shoulder, burning look and said, "What do you know, Eli?"

"Treat her right and Mr. Crubbsfeld might buy your college education." Eli slowed and nudged me with his elbow as though to say, just kidding. I shrank away from his touch and stayed quiet.

Joan lifted her chin defiantly and said, "I'm not going to college."

Eli seemed amused. "Oh you're not, huh?"

"Or finishing high school, either."

Eli gave a swift bark of laughter. Then he went strangely silent. He stopped walking and watched Joan carefully for a moment. "Joan," he said. It was funny to hear him sound so serious. "You're kidding, right?"

"Nope. I'm not. Not kidding at all." Joan kicked a rock. I watched it bound crookedly across the fake yellow bricks and onto a fake blue pool of water. "School is for people like you, and for people like Sunshine. It makes sense for you. You're good at it. Well, I'm not. Big fricking deal."

"Jesus, Joan, you really are stupid."

Joan stopped walking. "What did you say?"

"I said you're really horribly stupid. Grow up."

I pretended not to listen, trying to figure out what to do. Joan was upset: upset with me, upset with Eli, or just plain upset, I wasn't sure.

"Gawd," Joan bawled, "you're so mean!" She choked on her sobs and Eli came forward to comfort her. "I just figured that you would go to Gonzaga," she said, "and you would take care of me..."

The journey for cokes had definitely ended. I saw Eli's arm unwrap itself from Joan's heaving shoulders. I watched them with sick fascination, like they were two cars colliding.

"You're totally wrong," Eli said, trying to look her in the eyes. "I've never told you anything like that. We've never even done it!"

"I love you!" Joan screamed, sobbing. A few park customers gazed with curiosity at the spectacle. Eli was, of course, wearing his clown costume with the big, painted-on frown, although this was the first time I'd really seen him frowning in it. My heart went out to Joan.

"I better get back and check on The Rock 'N' Roller," I said stupidly.

Joan ignored me, but Eli said, "That's a good idea, Erin. Sorry about this."

Joan didn't return the whole night and wouldn't speak to me the next day. I wrung blisters into my hands and ached for some way to get back on her good side. The day after that, she was back to normal. I was so relieved when she smiled at me again and said, "Hi, Sunshine," that I almost fell on my knees.

After dinner one night, Dad swirled his whiskey and told me a few things about work. *You won't learn it in this job, Erin, but one day you'll see that being merciless is essential to success.*

Not long after Joan's meltdown, we were sitting together in one of the Rock 'N' Roller booths. The machine was set on the lowest speed so that the floor slowly rotated while Pantera wailed from the speakers.

Joan picked at the toe of her sneaker and commented, "This job is muy sucky."

"I dunno," I said, "it's not so bad."

Joan raised her head and studied me. Her eyes were kind.

"Your parents must have done a fricking job on you. What are they like?"

I shrugged. "My mom's pretty quiet, I guess. Dad's always talking. He's got a big voice. Sometimes I hear it ringing through my head, even when he's not around. He likes to say he's a predator."

"A predator?" Joan snorted. "That's classic." She pulled some lip-gloss from her pocket and applied it, then offered it to me. "Do you like them?"

"My parents?" I accepted the lip-gloss. "I love them."

"No, I know," Joan said, annoyed. "But do you like them? I mean, do you want to *be* like them?"

I considered this.

"I can't imagine being like my dad. But I don't know if that's because I don't like him or because I'm afraid of him."

"The predator," Joan mouthed thoughtfully. Then she leaned forward and dug her sharp fingernails into my knee. "If I tell you something," she said over the music, "keep it a secret."

I nodded, enraptured.

"I slept with Eli." She released me and leaned back with an air of triumph.

"Oh," I said. "Wow." I couldn't think of anything else to say except, "Good for you."

"Are you being mean?" Joan scowled at me. "Or are you being serious?"

"No," I said quickly. "Good for you. Truly."

"It was nothing." She lifted one shoulder and then dropped it, smiling with one side of her pretty mouth. I waited a moment while she gazed out at the earth revolving past us.

"So you're not mad at him anymore?"

"No." She shook her head. "All's good. I'm pretty sure we're on the same page now."

I hesitated. I tried to smile like the dark cloud hadn't been there, but she was already sitting up and asking, "What? What was that look for?"

"No," I said, "it's nothing. It's just… I don't know. What, exactly, is the same page?"

Joan stood and grasped the edge of the booth for balance. "I love him, okay? What's wrong with that?"

"Don't be mad at me. I'm happy for you. I'm really, really, really, happy for you."

I must have sounded insincere.

"I wouldn't expect such a Rich Prude to understand." She glowered at me. "You may not be as pretty as Alison, but you're just as much of a snob."

She stomped off the ride before I started crying. I'm sure that if Joan had seen me crying she would have apologized, as usual, and maybe what happened next would never have happened at all.

When someone approached the ticket console, I wiped at my face and walked tipsily across the floor. I leaped down so that I was next to the column, where the levers were, and then pulled The Rock 'N' Roller to a stop. I rearranged my face into fake cheer. The customer was a tall, handsome boy. I didn't recognize him at first.

It was Eli, without the clown get-up.

"Oh," I said, surprised. "Joan's out back, I think."

But then Joan was behind me. She gave my arm an angry little pinch.

"Hello, lover," she said to Eli, a greeting that made him squirm. "Geek-wad here thinks we're not on the same page."

He looked confused.

"Please don't bring me into this," I said meekly.

"Come here," she said to Eli, pulling him by the sleeve. "I want to talk to you." Then, in my ear she hissed, "About last night."

Her whole face became reptilian to me, all tense angles and slit eyes. The sun began to set. People milled peacefully about the park, some with their arms around one another's waists. And then there was Joan, with the lights of the Rock 'N' Roller casting her face purple and yellow and red. I wanted her to be pretty again, to convince Eli gently. But she looked like a 3-D version of the faces screaming on the large red column behind her. I visualized her floating up and into them, swallowed forever by rage and fear.

They stood beside one of the booths somewhat near me, although I could only hear what they were saying when they shouted. I wanted to turn down the music, thinking it would help to relieve some of the tension. Eli looked indifferent. He kept holding up his hands as she poked and prodded him.

Their conversation ended abruptly.

Joan burst into tears and gave Eli a resolute shove. He tripped backwards, overcorrected his balance, then fell face forward instead. Joan ran into the park's growing crowds and darkness. I shut off the Rock 'N' Roller lights and music, telling a couple of kids waiting impatiently at the ticket console to come back later. They flipped me the bird as they left.

"Are you okay?" I asked Eli. He was still lying on the floor. I assumed he was merely feeling overwhelmed with it all.

"I'm stuck," he said then. "My foot's stuck."

He was lying on his stomach, trying to twist his body around. His ankle was bent at an ugly angle. I wondered if it were broken. I leaned toward it and saw that his shoe was wedged between the layered plates of the rotating floor.

"Ouch," I said. "It'll come free if you take your shoe off."

"Well, I can't very well reach it, now can I?" Eli replied. He was too twisted around to sit up straight.

"Sorry," I said. "You want me to do it for you?"

"Yes," he grumbled. "Goddamn it."

I bent to take off the shoe, but then thought about Joan wandering broken-hearted through the park.

"Did you two break up?" I asked, hands hovering above his ankle.

"Erin," he said, "we were never even together. I never tried to pretend otherwise."

"I'm afraid if I let you go," I said, still crouching beside his feet, "you'll never come back to see her again."

"Why do you care?" Eli asked. "She's the one wasting her life. She wants to be trash and stay trash forever." He wriggled around on the floor. "Come on, please! The shoe!"

I rose, arguing, "I don't think she's trash. You should take that back."

"You're a goddamn saint, Erin," Eli practically frothed at the mouth. "And I don't get it, because she says the meanest shit about you."

I stepped off the floor and stood beside the operating panel in the middle of the red column. I wrapped my hand around one of levers and said, "You take it back, or I'll hit go."

"Just undo the shoe, you psycho."

I pressed the lever forward and he began rotating away from me.

"Stop it!" he shouted. "Stop it! Please, Erin, wait – "

The truth was, I wanted to scare him.

I wanted to scare him because I was scared of losing Joan and because I knew that Joan was scared of losing him. I could feel the fear in him then, when he said "Please," when he said, "Wait." I had already pulled the lever back into the stop position, but the floor was still moving, and I had forgotten about that one panel – the panel we were always warning the customers about tripping on, the panel that stuck out too far from the opposite end of the column – the panel that was now right in the way of Eli's head.

This is the thing I always remember, the thing I could never tell to Dad or to the police or to Gibbons and especially not to Joan, the thing that was too vivid for me to say out loud because it would show them the vastness of my regret: I heard a snap, like when Dad tore the leg off of an overcooked chicken, and the floor creaked to a stop. I went to look at him. His neck was awry, his tongue hung from his mouth like pink toffee. His eyes were wide and still. Everything I dreaded between hearing that sound and seeing those eyes simply was.

Eli was dead.

At the last moment he must have pulled free of the shoe. His socked foot rested beside his shoed foot. I shook him, still clinging to the hope that the nightmare would end, that he would sit up, grimacing and holding his head, and everything would be okay again. I grabbed his feet and pulled him with more strength than I knew I had across the Rock 'N' Roller floor, down the metallic steps, and onto the green pavement. I dropped his legs there and collapsed beside him. I rested my head on his outstretched arm and wept.

"That's muy shitty," Joan said. "Muy, muy fucked."

"No," I said, sitting up. "It's not what you think."

Joan laughed an evil witch's laugh. She came forward. "Your taste in women sucks, Eli," she said and kicked his socked foot. His head flopped around when she kicked him as though his spine had turned to wax. When he didn't respond she kicked harder. "Hey!" she screamed. "Hey, Eli!"

She noticed his eyes first. The color left her face.

"What?" she asked.

"He's dead," I told her. For some reason, I had stopped crying. These were now the facts. Joan's arrival had somehow severed the wires between the facts and my emotions. I continued, blandly, "He snapped his neck."

"Eli." She knelt beside him and poked him in the chest. "Eli," she whispered. Poke-poke. "Eli."

When she turned to puke, I went for the mop. I cleaned up after her while she mumbled incoherent, rambling sentences.

Finally she asked, "Where's his shoe?"

"It's stuck in The Rock 'N' Roller floor."

"How'd he snap his neck?"

"His foot was stuck. The floor rotated. His head struck that one panel."

Joan fumbled with her lip. She fumbled with Eli's lips. "He's so cold," she said.

"He's dead."

Joan nodded, sniffling. She rose and returned with Eli's shoe. She put it on his foot. "Like Cinderella," she said. She put her face in her hands and cried again.

I knew Gibbons would come looking for us. He'd wonder why The Rock 'N' Roller wasn't rockin' and rollin'. I almost giggled.

I said to her, "This is our fault. We killed him."

"I didn't kill him." Joan shook her head.

"None of this would have happened if his foot –"

"Why did you start it up?"

"I needed to," I sighed. "For the customers."

"There were customers?"

"No, but I thought I'd start it up. You know, to interest them."

Joan nodded. I had one mean, victorious thought that she wasn't as smart as I was, and then I retreated back into my fear and guilt.

"But the lights," she continued, "the music. They weren't on when I showed up."

For a second I thought I was caught.

"Well, of course not," I said slowly. "I'd found him by then, remember?"

"Oh, God," she said. "I'm going to be sick again."

Gibbons appeared, cursing and huffing. The three boys that had flipped me off followed at his heels. Had they seen everything? I started to my feet, ready to confess. I was going to admit that I had lied to Joan out of fear, but even if I hadn't lied it was still a horrible, freakish accident. But when Gibbons saw Eli's body lying there, he raised one large pink hand and the boys scattered like birds. Apparently they just wanted free rides. They had merely felt mistreated. For once I kept my big mouth shut.

Dad was adamant. *Of course it was an accident. You're a young girl and you don't know it yet, but time takes care of these things. In a couple of years, you'll barely remember what happened.*

Everyone else believed that, too: an accident. Gibbons even wondered that first night, gazing down at Eli's body, if I weren't covering for Joan. During the hearing, she sat regarding me with those slightly-crossed eyes that no longer gave her a look of innocence but rather a look of dumb fright. When Mr. Gunderson approached my parents and me, hand outstretched in forgiveness, Dad told me, *Stand up straight and stop whining.*

I accepted the hand and then a hug and wondered how Mr. Gunderson could feign such manliness.

I killed your son, I wanted to remind him. *That is not something you forgive.*

Mr. Gunderson did not offer the same warm hand or sweaty armpits to Joan.

I went up to her afterwards. She stared at me as though through a fog. She smelled of stale cigarettes.

"Hey." She asked, "How are you?"

"I'm okay," I said. "I feel really guilty."

It was the truth.

"Yaw," Joan said. "I hear that." She played with her lip, a nervous habit recently acquired, and said, "There's just some things that don't make sense. Why didn't he scream? Why didn't he call out to you?"

"The music," I said. "Or maybe, he was unconscious."

She glared at me. "That's what you said during the hearing. Word for word."

I swallowed a lump in my throat.

"You're my only friend," I told her.

I just wanted to scare him. That's all. For you. All for you.

"I can't think about this anymore," she said. "Maybe I'll see you when school starts."

On the way home Dad was almost lachrymose. *It's a tragedy when such a young man dies before fulfilling his potential.*

Joan must have switched schools. I only saw her once more, years later. I was interning for my father's company the summer after my first year of college. Dad and I walked down a street in downtown Spokane.

He was showing me a building that he might tear down for new condominiums. Joan was there, sitting on the steps of the building, smoking a cigarette. She gazed up at us with those funny, crisscrossed eyes.

"Hi, Joan," I said. My stomach somersaulted.

"Oh hey," she drawled. "It's you." She studied my father and me, and then grimaced. "Sunshine and the Predator."

Dad clutched me by the elbow and steered me into the building. *That type of woman is always on drugs.*

I shook my arm free of him. I went back outside. Joan had crossed the street. I could see the curves of her shoulders bobbing away from me, disappearing around a corner. I started following her, but the light changed. The cars accelerated. I was stuck. It was useless. We were all stuck.

I reentered the building and overheard Dad speaking with another man in a business suit. *It helps in this business to be merciless.* Dad turned and saw me standing there. *Oh, here's my daughter now,* he said. *Come here, Erin.*

The man in the business suit extended his hand. He smiled at me with perfect white teeth. To my father, he said, "The resemblance is uncanny."

vvvvvvvvvvvvvvvvvvvvvvvvvv

MORSELS

∧∧∧∧∧∧∧∧∧∧∧∧∧∧∧∧∧∧∧∧∧∧∧∧∧∧

I'm afraid of death. I thought of this while I was watching a movie last night, but not because the movie made death seem like a scary thing, rather it seemed like a glorious, glorified thing, and what scares me is that it won't be glorious or glorified at all – just nothing, just death. This bothers me because I'm a claustrophobic. I don't like the idea of being stuck anywhere. I would rather be in hell. Because even though they all say that hell sucks, that there's nothing decent going on there, I'll bet you a trillion dollars that every once in a while you'll be resting on your pitchfork, taking a slight break while The Whipmaster sips at his coffee, and you'll look out over the valleys and hills of hell and think, hey, fire and brimstone are sort of pretty at this hour, almost like a big, violent sunset. And right before The Whipmaster takes up his whip and starts clobbering your back again, you'll think, hey, even those baby-heads, the baby-heads that have no bodies – just wings where their necks used to be – even those baby-heads floating around biting people can be pretty cute sometimes. That doesn't sound so bad. If you're conscious enough to at least have thoughts, then I'm sure no matter how horrible things got, there would still be some goodness there, and sometimes I'll bet that goodness would almost make everything seem worth it. Even when damned for all eternity.

This is why I took that job as a butcher. I've been looking for mortal answers. There's something about working with large slabs of meat that's illuminating. I mean, these slabs used to be alive. In the mornings, brushing my teeth, I'll picture the skin peeling away. I've heard that sheep are stupid animals, not very self-aware. I wouldn't mind coming back as one for that very reason.

The other day a woman asks for a lamb shank. I go to carve the meat for her, and as I'm carving, I'm thinking about how little Lambert was probably skippity-dooing just the day before, until he was herded up with the others in a barn and shot smack between the eyes. I got to feeling really sorry for the thing, because now it was going to be sold to some fatso woman in a paisley dress, bustled home to her four blotchy, screaming children, only to be pooped out by the whole miserable family the next day. The lamb was pink and warm in my hands. I almost cried.

I turned and told the woman, "We're out of lamb shank."

"You just said you had it."

"No, I'm sorry. We're out."

Her fat mouth twisted up. "Well then what, young lady, were you cutting at just now?"

"I thought it was lamb shank, but it's not. It's the lamb's gut, I think."

She rose on her tiptoes and peered at the meat in my hands. "That's fine," she said. "That's fine, I'll take that."

I looked down, confused. "It's not lamb," I said, "it's bear."

She grimaced. "Bear?"

"Yes, I'm sorry. Bear. The butt, I believe. Or the intestines or the spleen or something."

"That," she said, pointing a sausagey finger, "is not bear. And it's certainly not intestine or spleen."

"This isn't even meat," I said, "this is like that tofu-ish meat. Tofurkey or Tobear or Tolamb or something? It's not very good for you. They douse it in pig's blood, to make it look more real."

"I'm telling the manager," she said.

Carl asked me later to go home, but his voice wasn't angry, just sleepy.

I took the meat home with me. I figured, if someone's going to eat this meat, it should be someone that's deeply, importantly afraid of her own mortality. It was tasty enough. But after a few bites, the meat began loping about in my stomach. I clutched my gut and went to the toilet and heaved. Each morsel had turned into a little red lamb, complete with a head and legs and hooves and eyeballs and everything. They galloped frantically around the bowl of the toilet, skirting the water's edge. One of the braver morsels ducked its head and lapped at the water. I felt sorry for the whole lot of them, but there really wasn't anything to be done. Where would I keep them? In an aquarium? A hamster cage? They were marbled and dripping. Despite their playfulness, they were hideous.

"All things must come to an end," I said.

And then I flushed.

vvvvvvvvvvvvvvvvvvvvvvvvv

PULCHRITUDINOUS

∧∧∧∧∧∧∧∧∧∧∧∧∧∧∧∧∧∧∧∧∧∧∧∧∧

Bea's in trouble. There's new management, run by Mr. Sneezbee. He doesn't like "Monkey Business." We all have to wear matching vests, name-tags shaped like explosives, maroon visors like we're working in fast food. More often than not Bea forgets an accessory or two. Mr. Sneezbee also makes everyone, even the people who have worked at Foodbomb for a grillion years, attend a once-a-month class on how to become a "Superlative Customer Service Representative," which is, frankly, a joke. We're all getting paid minimum wage, so what kind of quality can they expect? The meetings are boring and sometimes cruel. Mr. Sneezbee is always demoting people for things they've neglected to do. Bea is his favorite victim. For some reason he loves me. Always tells me I'm going places. It's funny, too, because he's so serious all the time, but then he tells me to call him, please, Alex. Which I won't do. He's too much like a teacher or something.

At the Superlative Customer Service meetings, whenever Mr. Sneezbee begins cutting people down, I stop listening and gaze out the conference window. It's on the second floor with the other offices, and the window provides a view of the entire store. Foodbomb is strange without people. The walls are pink and the carpet red, and it's the size of a small airport. Sometimes I peer at the canned vegetables and try to imagine which one of them contains a factory worker's fingernail, which one a rat's tail. You know with all of those cans that there has to be one that's a mess inside. One that will be opened up and thrown away. The defective one.

The best thing about this job is that Mr. Sneezbee lets us take home magazines for free but with the covers torn off. My favorite is a fashion magazine – *Pulchritudinous*. I showed it to Simone once, and she said, wrinkling her nose, "What's that mean?" and I said, "It means beautiful," and she said, "That's an ugly word for beautiful." We shared a candy bar in the sunshine. It melted onto our fingers. We left greasy prints on all of the pages, ranking the models by who was the most pulchritudinous, who was the least. Mom saw the magazine and frowned. "Those models look malnourished." Simone and I examined the pages. "But," Simone argued, "it's the *fashion* that counts." Mom said she didn't care much for fashion and then disappeared back inside the house. Simone sucked on her lip and then suggested, "Maybe that's why your Dad left her for the cigarette lady," and I shrugged. "Maybe," I said. But I think it had more to do with his being selfish.

Anyway, I guess my point here is, talking about these magazines and cans and stuff, is that I space out, too. Just like Bea. She doesn't bother me so much. The only time she ever annoys me is when someone like Simone will come through for a pack of gum and a Gatorade. Simone eyes Bea over like she's a beast from the wilderness and raises her eyebrows at me as though to say, "Jeez, who stuck you with the Beast of the Wilderness?" I get uncomfortable because half-of-me wants to laugh and the other half-of-me wants to tell Simone to grow up. Or Roger will come through for a pack of cigs and Bea will say something like, "Are you sure he's seventeen?" and I'll say, "Oh yeah, sure, he's a year older than me, I know him from school," even though he's not a year older than me, and even though it's illegal. I always have to look around to make sure management didn't hear her.

So yeah, she's spacey, but I still like her. I would rather be stuck with Bea than with crotchety Mr. Ford, who never forgets to ask paper or plastic but who also tattle-tales on everyone, even on himself. Bea's better than him any day, slow and forgetful as she is.

Bea's always asking me, "Hey Cindy, mind if I take a break?"

I always say, "Sure, please, go ahead."

The lines move faster when I do my own bagging, anyway.

It's hot outside and slow inside. In between customers, Bea leans her soft elbows on the space where people write checks and watches me count bills.

She suddenly just blurts out, "I wish I was like you."

I raise my eyebrows at her.

"I mean I wish I'd been more like you. When I was younger. You know?"

"What are you talking about?" I roll my eyes. "My life totally sucks."

Bea shrugs. I shove the bills into the security bag and tuck it under the register. "Maybe," she says. "Maybe your life sucks, but you handle it better. Better than me, better than I did."

"Bea," I say, wiping a droplet of sweat from my temple, "it couldn't have been that bad."

Her voice is drippy, sweet like syrup, but sad and slow, too. "Oh, I don't know. It wasn't all bad. I got voted 'Best Smile' in high school. That was nice."

I chuck her on the shoulder. "There, I can totally see that. Really."

Bea nods, brightens for a moment. "Well, it was a small school. Small town. But I was liked alright. At school, anyway." Her face goes gray again.

I study Bea a little sadly. She has large wet patches growing in the purple armpits of her shirt. She is looking down at her hands, plump fingers thrust together on the check stand, and she has a staircase of fat that falls from her chin to her chest. I agree with her old classmates: the nicest thing about her looks is her smile, which lights up her eyes and irons out her wrinkles, but right now she is frowning. I try to think of something to cheer her up. Mr. Ford walks by with some carts. I say to him, "Hey, Lover," and give him a big, theatrical wink. Bea smirks at me. Mr. Ford gives me a confused look, adjusts his Foodbomb visor, and then tells me to go eat turds.

"Don't be fooled," I say to Bea, who clutches her thick middle and doubles over laughing, "he really loves me. I can't wait for our wedding night."

"Better bring…" she says, sputtering with laughter, "better bring…"

"What?" I say, and I'm laughing now too, just because it's contagious.

"The Viagra!"

And she howls.

I say through my laughter, "Wow, Bea, you made a joke! I'm impressed!"

Mr. Sneezbee materializes out of nowhere. He puts his white knuckles against his hips without balling his fists, and opens his eyes wide at us. "You two having a good time?" he asks.

We sober up and stand at attention. He looks Bea over and nods at her armpits. "Looks like you've been doing manual labor. Why don't you go towel off?"

Bea lowers her head and moves off toward the bathrooms. I wince looking at her, because her Foodbomb vest is tucked into her underwear, and you can see it riding above the wide black sweatpants she always wears. Mr. Sneezbee shakes his head.

"Can you believe the old owners hired such a monster?" he says, disgusted.

I don't respond, just hand him the cash bag. "It's all counted, Mr. Sneezbee."

He takes the bag from me and looks at me as though he has never seen me before in his whole stupid life. "Listen, Cindy," he says, "just between you and me. There're some big changes coming to this store. Big changes. Huge ones. Let me ask you one thing: are you ready for them?"

I shrug. "Sure. Yeah."

"That's what I like to hear. That's what I love to hear!" He turns to the nearly empty aisles and spreads open his arms and shouts, "Everyone, Cindy is READY!"

A couple of customers push their carts around.

"Well, Cindy," he says, putting one arm around my shoulders and leaning in so that I can smell his sour breath, "just between you and me, Bea is not ready for those changes."

"No?"

"No. Definitely not ready." He straightens, surveys the store like he's on top of a mountain. "Nope. Definitely. Not at all."

A customer shoves her cart up to my register. I gratefully begin running her purchases through. "I forgot my Foodbomb card," she says in a tired voice. "Can I just give you my phone number?"

I say no problem. Mr. Sneezbee stands there, watching me ten-key and nodding like he's proud of me. I tell the woman, "You saved twenty-five cents today. Thank you for shopping Foodbomb."

And as she walks off Mr. Sneezbee says, patting my arm and turning to leave, "Cindy, you could be like a daughter to me," which makes me cringe. I haven't seen my dad since he ditched Mom and me for the woman who sold cigarettes and magazines on the corner of 4th and Pine. That was two years ago. He sent me a postcard from Las Vegas for Christmas last year, saying how big of a heart I have, despite my sarcastic mouth. He always said that kind of stuff. It was tacky, sending me a postcard like that, but it made me miss him. Or miss something. But that something certainly isn't Mr. Sneezbee, with his raunchy breath and squeaky shoes.

Bea returns as I'm running another customer through. Mr. Sneezbee stands there as though waiting for her to make a mistake, but she even remembers to ask paper or plastic, and to be extra delicate with the eggs.

Simone asks if I can stay the night. Mom says no, but that Simone's welcome to stay at our place. Simone agrees and I hang up the phone. I've been staying at Simone's a lot lately. Mom's kind of tired of it. But I like Simone's house. It's really clean, as though a magic oilcloth descends from the sky once an hour to wipe away every speck of dust. And they've got nicer things. Breakable things and leather couches. They also have a dog that doesn't smell like constant farts all the time. I tell Mom this.

"You love Rufus," she grins, "don't deny it." And then she says, leaning forward to eat the peas I've ignored on my plate, "You shouldn't compare yourself to Simone all the time. You've got great qualities, things she'll never have."

"Thank you, oh great seer," I say.

Mom laughs. "You know what your father used to say about you?"

I know. But I don't stop her.

"That despite your sarcastic mouth, you've got an enormous heart."

I scoop my peas onto her plate. Rufus comes into the room, drooling and panting and smelling like farts. "That means a lot coming from a man with *no* heart," I say. "And no brain, for that matter."

Mom tells me what she always tells me, that I should learn to forgive, that I should understand that he loves me, that eventually I'll be ready for him to come back into my life, just in a different form. I nod and twirl my hair and let her eat my peas and blab. Then I go into the other room to read the latest issue of *Pulchritudinous*. Mom comes in and tells me to get my feet off of the coffee table.

"Those women look malnourished," she repeats.

"I know, Mom," I say. "They're on a strict diet of water and peas."

Mom smirks and squeezes my toes. Rufus wanders into the living room, looking for me as always. He drops his woolly head onto my knee. I massage his ears while I read about weight loss and vagina exercises. I haven't had sex yet, but I figure it doesn't hurt to prepare.

The doorbell rings. It's Simone. She kisses my cheek as she always does when she sees me (she thinks it's very European) and then says, "What smells like farts?"

"Oh," I say, "I was just petting the dog."

"You should wash your hands," she suggests.

So I do.

It's Friday and Foodbomb's packed. I'm running people through as quickly as possible, but they keep coming, their loaded carts snaking into aisle seven – Babies/Medicines/Feminine Products. When I'm waiting for people to finish signing their checks, I can hear Bea huffing and whining at my side.

"Bea," I say, "don't have a heart attack."

"No, I'm fine," she says, trying with her thick fingers to be delicate with the eggs. "I'm fine."

Simone comes through the line. She gives me that look again as I ring up her pack of gum. The *What's-With-the-Beast* look.

"A quarter," I say.

"Hey," she says, "last night was fun."

"Yeah," I say, waiting for the frigging quarter, because the truth is, last night was not fun. In short, it consisted of Simone mooning over Roger, scribbling on the back of an old math assignment her first name coupled with his last name as she asked me question after question about them: do you think I should sleep with him, do you think we'd have cute babies, could you see us married some day, do you think he looks like a younger version of my dad, blab, blab, blab. What's funny though is that when she finally got up the balls to call him, he asked to talk to me. And when I hung up, grinning and feeling like my cheeks were all hot, she asked, "What did he say about me?" For the first time in my life I felt like spitting on my palm and rubbing it into the perfect round nub of her nose. But of course, I didn't.

And now I say, "Last night was a lotta fun."

"Roger invited us, you know," she says. "Swimming tomorrow. He told me he really wants you to come, too."

She holds the quarter in her hand but doesn't hand it over. Bea shuffles and coughs at my side. I can't tell if Simone is angry about what Roger said or not.

"Well, yeah, but I've gotta work." All I want is for Simone to leave so that I can get through the grillion-and-one customers. "So I can't go."

Simone looks at me, then at Bea. She pouts. "Oh, too bad. Work. I forgot," and hands me the quarter. "Woulda been fun, though."

She prances off, then turns and shouts, "I'll call you tonight, okay Cindy?" And I realize that she's not insinuating anything at all. She would never suspect that Roger would ever be interested in me.

Bea asks me for the next hour if I'm okay. I keep shrugging. Finally, after the umpteenth time, I tell her to please leave me alone, I mean look at all these people for crissakes and Bea would you please just remember to ask them what kind of bag they want, jeez! She settles down and remembers to ask. Then I hear her sniffling. I avoid looking at her, but I feel bad. A woman comes through the line and asks Bea if she's crying.

"Allergies," Bea lies.

While I wait for the woman to finish writing her check, I pass Bea a Kleenex. She blinks at me, grateful. I hand the woman her Foodbomb card and tell her, "You saved nineteen cents today, Miss Evers. Thank you for shopping Foodbomb." Bea stops sniffling.

A couple of customers later, she drops the eggs.

The customer stops talking on his cell phone long enough to scream at me, "Did you know how long I've been waiting in line?"

Bea goes to collect more eggs, muttering self-deprecating curses as she slinks away. I try to calm the man down.

"I'll give you the eggs for free," I assure him.

"Big fucking deal!" He shrieks, "That's like fifty cents!" He stops shrieking and brings the phone to his ear and says, "Listen, I've got a major situation here. The employees at Foodbomb are trying to ruin my life."

I wipe up the mess on the counter. I pretend the man is not there.

"Why do they hire inept employees?" he asks the person behind him, who shrinks away from him as though afraid she'll get punched.

Bea lumbers back. She bags the man's goods, and he pays, and I am just about to tell him that he's saved twelve cents, plus his free eggs, when he leans close to Bea's face and tells her, "You are a worthless, stupid old cunt."

Bea opens and closes her mouth. The man begins to walk off, but I shout at him, "You forgot your Foodbomb card!" and when he turns back toward me, his face twisting with fresh rage, I flick the card to the floor and say, "Pick it up yourself, asshole."

Someone in line snickers. The man points at the card. He is well off, you can tell by the clothes, by the fancy hair and shoes, and he's used to getting his way.

He points at the card. "Give it to me," he snarls. "Right now."

"No," I say, and when Bea, frightened, bends to retrieve it, I put my hand on her shoulder and tell her, "No."

I can tell how steady my own hands are as Bea trembles within her vest.

Mr. Ford comes over, and trailing behind him, rising on his tiptoes to see over Mr. Ford's high shoulder, is Mr. Sneezbee.

"What is going on here?" Mr. Sneezbee demands.

"Your staff is rude and incompetent," the man says. His face is bright red, as if blood is about to shoot from his tiny ears. "I fully expect some heads to roll here."

Mr. Ford says, pointing at Bea and I, "I saw her, she threw the card at him."

"Bea!" scolds Mr. Sneezbee. "I should have known that this woman would be capable of such a cruel, cold, senseless thing as throwing objects at customers. Bea, if you would follow me to the office please, and if you could hand me your Foodbomb visor, oh I see you've forgotten that again, no surprise there, and, well, I'll need your Foodbomb vest and please your Foodbomb nametag…"

Bea begins unbuttoning her vest but Mr. Ford shakes his head. "No," he says. "Not Bea. The brat. You know, Cindy. Chucked it at his feet."

Mr. Sneezbee frowns.

"It's true sir," I say, "or almost anyway. I didn't throw it at him. I sorta threw it at the floor."

"On accident?" Mr. Sneezbee asks, brightening.

"No. Not really. More like on purpose."

I lean in and explain what the man said to Bea.

"What?"

"Stupid old cunt," I repeat.

"Well," Mr. Sneezbee says. "Well."

He looks a little confused, and I'm thinking, for crissakes do you really hate Bea so much that you'll let this asshole get away with that? And then I'm also thinking about what they tell us at our Superlative Customer Service Meetings, that no matter what, even if someone shits in the bill of your Foodbomb visor and puts it back on your head, you're supposed to do everything you can to make them happy. Money is money and assholes have money, too, so if shitting in the bill of your Foodbomb visor makes the customer happy, then go ahead and let them shit there and management promises not to take out of your salary the amount for a new Foodbomb visor. That's the general gist of it, anyway. So, given that gist, I can practically guess what Mr. Sneezbee will say next.

"My employee begs your forgiveness, sir. And if you would please follow me to my offices I will gladly make out a Foodbomb gift certificate for the amount of fifteen – no, make that twenty – Foodbomb dollars, to use on whatever purchases you require."

"Alright," the man says. His cell phone rings. "Sounds okay, I guess." And then, to the cell phone, "Situation solved. Let's talk dinner."

They walk away, the man chatting and throwing his hands around, his groceries still sitting on the floor.

Mr. Sneezbee returns several minutes later. "Why don't you take the weekend off, Cindy? To cool down. We'll talk Monday."

"But I – "

"I don't want you working here until we sit down and really discuss what transpired here today. And today, well, I'm frankly just too disappointed."

"Fine with me," I say, "see ya." And walking out into the bright sunlight I remember chatting on the phone last night with Roger, and I think, yeah, who cares, tomorrow I'm going swimming.

The next morning I wait for Simone to pick me up. Mom lets Rufus out. He puts his farty smelling head on my leg and I think, Great, now Roger's going to smell fart all over me, and I am about to get up and change my pants when the city bus pulls up across the street. A large purple form stumbles from it and ambles hesitantly toward my house. Toward me.

"Bea," I say, alarmed. Great, I think, Simone will never let this die. "What are you doing here?"

"Oh, Cindy," she says, "I had to talk to you."

I sit back down and Rufus puts his stinking head on my lap again. Bea reaches out to pet him and says, "Nice doggie." I ask her what's up.

"I needed to thank you for what you did for me," Bea says. "What you did yesterday. I mean, nobody, nobody Cindy, has ever done something like that for me before."

A car cruises down the street. I rise on my heels to see who it is. It's not them. I sit back down, relieved.

"No, Bea, it's no problem. That guy was a jerk."

Bea wrings her hands. I'm glancing at her and then at the street. Please, I think, let them be super late.

Her eyes watch me and fill with worry. "Cindy, what if they fire you? It would be all my fault. Terrible, terrible of me."

"You know Bea," I say, "I'm alright if they fire me. Foodbomb sucks. It would be an honor to get fired from there."

"But you'd have to find another job!" she protests. "And we'd never get to work together again!"

She's taking this really hard, nearly crying right there on my freaking porch, and just as I wrap one arm around her shoulders, someone honks. I look up and there is Simone, sitting in the passenger seat of Roger's car. Someone else sits in the back seat. Alan, Roger's best friend. I raise my hand to them. "One minute!" I call.

"Bea," I say, giving her shoulders a quick squeeze before releasing her. "Get a hold of yourself, okay?"

Her gasping slows. She wipes at her eyes and squints into the sun. "I'm okay," she says. "It's just, you're my only friend. And maybe I ruined your life."

I force a laugh. Why won't she leave? I can feel a flush creeping up my chest and neck. "You didn't ruin my life! Do you really think Sneezbee will fire me because of this? No way!"

A door pocks shut. Roger walks up to the porch. "Everything okay?" he asks.

"Yeah," I say, "everything's fine."

Roger stares at Bea.

"Oh," I say, "Bea, this is Roger. Roger, this is Bea. I work with her. At Foodbomb."

"Cool," he says. He tugs at my elbow and at the bottom of the steps he asks me how old Bea is. I tell him like a grillion years old. He asks old enough to buy alcohol and I say yes.

"Hey Bea," he says. She looks at us expectantly, as does Rufus. "How would you like to go swimming?"

Bea looks at me hesitantly. Roger is grinning full wattage. I tell her hollowly, "Okay, yeah. Sure. Bea, come on. It'll be great."

Bea doesn't notice my unenthused tone. She breaks into a large, attractive smile. "Great. Yes! I mean, if I'm not intruding. I haven't been swimming in ages."

"Cool," Roger says. He grins at me. "We'll stop by a drugstore and pick up some beer."

Bea looks hesitant at this last statement, but Roger acts all charming, opening the door for her with a flourish, and making Alan crush into the hatchback so that we "ladies" will have ample room. Bea says something about not having a bathing suit and everyone laughs. She looks at me. I smile at her, but at the same time I'm thinking, Alright now you *are* a Beast of the Wilderness, and now you *are* ruining my life. My neck and chest and cheeks are blotchy red. Simone has to point this out to everyone.

"You look sunburnt," she says.

"No," Bea says in my defense. "She looks like she's wearing blush. She looks lovely. Everyone thinks Cindy is the prettiest employee at Foodbomb. Prettier than any of the customers even!"

Roger catches my eye in the rearview mirror. Now I really am blushing. "I can see that," he says. "I can see that, definitely."

From the hatchback, Alan whines, "My neck is cramping up back here! There's no space and it's hot!"

"It's so great for you guys to have me," Bea chatters. "I really love being around people, and you guys are all so young and nice and smart, it's really a pleasure for me."

I press my forehead against the window and feel like I'm dying a slow death from heat stroke and mortification.

"That's really nice of you, Bea," Simone gushes, sounding genuine. I can't tell if she's mocking Bea or not.

"Yeah," Alan says. "Real nice! And nice of you to buy us alcohol! For the love of Christ, Roger, could you crank the air conditioner?"

"No," Roger says. "It kills the ozone layer."

Roger asks Bea if she's comfortable. "More than ever," she replies. Everyone laughs again, as if this is hilarious.

We're both being mocked to death. Like birds pecking at us. Bea, though, seems to love every second of it.

When we pull away from the drugstore, beer and wine with Alan in the back, Simone cranes her neck to look at me from the front seat.

"You smell like farts again," she says. "Forget to wash your hands?"

This time, Bea has nothing to say in my defense.

They get drunk. Even Bea. Roger acts all charming with her, and when she gets on the diving board and jumps into the empty pool he and Alan scream with laughter. Alan slaps his thighs and hoots, "Delicious! Delicious!" as Bea struggles to the surface in the monstrous dark tent of her clothes. They tell her they're impressed that she's the first one in the water.

"I always was first when I was young, boys," she crows. "I was famous for it!"

I sit at the edge of the pool with my feet in the water, holding a bottle of wine on my lap. It's red wine, warm and thick, and after one sip I know I can't drink it. I hold it to me, anyway, for comfort. It makes me look like I'm having fun. The boys strip down to nothing and jump in at the same time. They leer at Simone and me. It's so hot out that I can't sit directly on the pavement, so I sit on a cushion stolen from a lounge chair. The sun glints off of the flakes of water, turning them white like snow as they spin into the air. Bea pulls a bottle of wine and a yellow inner tube into the pool and floats there, drinking and murmuring how happy she is. The boys take turns chugging beer and then springing off the diving board. They serve beer to Simone and Bea. I refuse, lifting my full bottle of wine and saying, flirtatiously, "Sorry boys, I'm busy," although I'm not busy, I'm just upset. Simone, after her fourth beer, speedily sheds her shorts, tank top and fancy black sandals. Naked, she executes a nervous little dance over to the edge of the pool, pretending to concentrate on Bea, who is attacking her own bottle

113

of wine and shouting about how she's never truly been drunk before, and how wonderful it feels.

"We're so alive right now," she shouts. "I'm really still young, if you think about it."

Every now and then she turns to me and lifts the bottle, saluting. I smile at her and wish she weren't here. Simone swims naked in the water with the boys. They are all too nervous to glance at one another. They laugh at me for having my clothes on. Even Bea gets out and suddenly strips. She cannonballs into the water and someone shouts, "Look at her go!" I try not to look but can't help it. She's huge, torpedoing below the surface with rolls of fat and stringy brown hair wiggling around her, but at the same time, I think she looks placid, happy. Not ugly at all. She even looks agile.

"Hippos can swim, right?" Roger asks me. "I guess there's proof."

"Hush," I say. "She'll hear you."

"Don't get me wrong. I really like her."

I roll my eyes at him.

He says, "I do. Now get in the water."

"No."

"Take off your clothes."

"Not yet."

"Have a beer."

I accept a beer. Just one. Right as I finish it, Bea suddenly heaves up and out of the water, lurches toward the locker rooms. She can barely walk. Simone's laughing with the boys about something, arms folded over her breasts. Roger keeps swimming around me, humming. I catch a glimpse of his small, flat butt. His tiny pecker. I don't feel all that impressed, but I like that he's drifting around me, instead of around Simone. I close my eyes and lean back. I'm so hot. I'm melting.

"Lesbian lovers!" Simone says. "That's what they looked like, standing on her porch: weirdo lesbian lovers!"

I lift up. The boys are laughing at me. "Suck it, Simone," I mumble.

"No, it's true! Dontcha think? Roger? Rogey? Dontcha think?"

He cocks his head and looks at me. "Yeah, maybe." He grins. "Maybe."

"Jeez," I say, and stand up and pull my tank top over my head, and then I lower my shorts and underwear and am standing there. I'm not nervous. I don't dance around like Simone. I think about what my mom said. I have things Simone doesn't have. I'm sure of it now. I've got Roger, for example. And Simone knows it. That's why she's been so mean lately. It's transparent now, now that she's drunk. And I've got a taller body, better legs. I stand there and make everyone else nervous. Then I dive into the water and swim right up to Roger and kiss him on the mouth with my tongue waggling and everything. I turn to Simone, whose jaw has dropped, and I say, "A lesbian, huh?" The boys laugh and Simone mutters something. I swim away. From the shade beneath the diving board, I see Roger looking ridiculous, ashamed. All of them, Alan, Roger, Simone, look stupid and young. I'm bored with all of them.

I get out of the pool and go to the locker rooms. I look for Bea. She's not there. I find a stall and pee and let the sunspots fade from my vision a bit. When I leave the stall, I try to rinse the beer taste from my mouth with tap water. I want to find Bea and get her home. I walk outside and hear a lot of noise coming from the men's locker room.

"Bea?" I ask from the doorway.

"Hey Cindy, come here," Alan says. "You'll love this."

"Look, is Bea in there? I want to go home."

"Yeah, she's here," says Roger. "Come here."

I enter. We're all naked. Simone, Alan, Roger, Bea and I. Bea is a large fleshy lump on the floor. She's on her side, lying in her own puke. She keeps bubbling puke out of her mouth. I feel so bad that I want to sit beside her on the floor and stroke her head. She groans and pukes again.

"We should clean her off," Simone suggests.

"With what?" Roger says, looking around. "A hose? A bucket?"

"A hose," Alan snickers. "Check this shit out!"

And he yanks on his pecker and aims the thin stream at Bea. Roger starts in, too, and they egg one another on, pissing on her chest and stomach. Alan aims at her sagging breasts. Simone says, "Ew, gross, you guys," and leaves, but for some reason I can't. I tell them to stop it, but they are laughing so hard that it feels contagious. Suddenly I'm laughing too because, Jeez, look at her, she's just lying there taking this shit. As they laugh the pee squirts jerkily on and off, which makes us laugh harder.

"Oh, Jesus," Roger says. "I got some in her hair."

"Raunchy!" Alan says. "Watch, I'm gonna spell my name on her belly."

"That won't show up dude," protests Roger, but he's laughing anyway.

Alan tries to spell his name but can't. "Fuck, I'm all peed out."

"Me, too," says Roger. "But you know who ain't?" And he thumbs at me, hitchhiker style.

"Come on, Cindy!" Alan urges. "Spell your name on her!"

"Like Etch a Sketch," Roger says.

"No way." I shake my head, watching Bea for movement.

"She'll do it," Roger slurs drunkenly. He gazes at me with pure affection. "She'll do it. That's why she's so much cooler than Simone, that tight-ass." I stand there, hesitating. "Or is Bea your lesbian lover, after all?"

"Well," I say, hesitating. "I'll feel bad."

"Oh, she's so passed out she'll never know," Roger insists. "Not at all. She'll still worship you, I promise."

I crouch over her head. It's the narrowest part, and I don't want to spread my legs very far. I piss right onto her nose. I think about what my Dad said to me, before he left, when I was crying and telling him that I hated him for loving someone else, for hurting us. He said, "I can't be mad at myself for the things that I've done. Life is too short. You'll have to forgive me, too." But I never did. Not even close.

I stop peeing but am still crouching slightly when I see one of Bea's eyes squinting up at me.

"Oh no," I say.

"What?" Alan asks.

The boys are slapping one another on their naked backs, as though they've scored a touchdown. They stop congratulating one another and come over to stand by my side.

"She saw me."

"She did not. I was watching her face the whole time. She didn't see shit." Roger puts his arm around my shoulder.

"One eye opened," I say. I peer down into her face, shrugging his arm off of me.

"Hey, what gives?" he says, hurt.

Her eyes are certainly closed now. For a moment I hope she is dead.

"Nah," Alan says, "she didn't even blink. We were both watching."

"I'm calling a cab," I say. My knees are trembling. "I'm going home."

"Wait," Roger says, "let me give you a ride."

"No," I say, "I'm going to be sick." I sprint outside and puke into the pool.

Simone comes up to me, fully dressed now, and holds my hair away from my face.

"You okay?" she asks and I tell her no, that I'm leaving. "I'm coming, too," she says. I cry a little bit while I'm pulling on my clothes.

Simone says, considering me, "What, Roger doesn't like you? Big deal. He doesn't like me, either. Don't feel so bad."

In the cab, Simone sighs and says, "I can't believe what those boys did that to that poor woman."

I don't respond.

"I thought she was pretty cool, you know? I mean, not many adults can party with kids like that. And she was pretty brave, getting naked and all."

"She wasn't brave. She was drunk."

"Well, at the very least she was super-nice." She leans her head back on the seat and sighs. "God, I feel sick."

I think of Bea rising hours later, naked and alone, maybe even prodded awake by the mop of some late-night janitor. I try to think of what that would feel like, waking up abandoned and naked.

"I'm an asshole," I say aloud, to no one.

"No you're not," Simone says, startling me. "You're my best friend."

This assertion makes me want to cry all over again, but I don't. Simone lays her head against my shoulder and moans that she has the spins. Outside, the world darkens, the horizon laced by purple night. The cab drops Simone off first.

Once home, I rinse the vomit from my mouth. Mom opens the door to my room and lays the new issue of *Pulchritudinous* on my bed. She asks me if I'm okay. "Sun-sick," I say, and she pets my head for a moment before leaving. Later, Rufus noses the door open and flops onto my bed, too. I bury my hand in his fur and fall back asleep, even though his smell makes my eyes water.

Bea calls in sick to work for almost a full week. I arrive at Foodbomb both relieved and annoyed to find her missing. I both want and don't want to speak with her.

Then, one morning, she's there. She smiles at me meekly and says hello. She's forgotten, again, her Foodbomb visor. Everything seems spot-on normal.

I'm not sure if I should mention the other day. I know that she won't if I don't. And maybe, I think, she doesn't remember anything after all. Maybe I imagined it: the opening eyeball. Guilt, or something.

When I first returned to work on Monday, Mr. Sneezbee called me into his office to talk about "the incident." He told me that while my behavior was understandable, it certainly wasn't acceptable, and that in the end it simply wasn't worth it to lose a valuable customer due to his – and my –

crankiness. He went on to say that I was forgiven and that I wouldn't be fired, but that if any other mishap occurred you'd better believe that my name would come up in the Superlative Customer Service meetings. I didn't say a word the whole time, because I was thinking about how inconsistent I am, how in between Friday and Saturday I had gone from defending a nice albeit geeky woman to peeing on her face. Dad always talks about my big heart, but now I'm realizing what a further sign of his idiocy that is.

I'm hanging out with Roger and Simone later today. We're giving Rufus a bath. Simone's idea. I sort of don't want Simone finding out about my peeing on Bea. I think it would give her something else to hold over me. But I think it's cool that Simone didn't do it. It makes me prouder of her. Less proud of me.

Today, Bea keeps forgetting to ask paper or plastic. It surprises me, because she was getting so much better about it, but once again, I'm asking for her.

"Can I go on break?" Bea asks me.

"Of course," I say. "Go ahead."

She leaves. Mr. Ford comes up to help me bag. He's in a crotchety mood, as always.

"You know," he tells me, "Bea wasn't really sick."

I tell a customer how much she saved with her Foodbomb card. "Thanks for shopping Foodbomb."

"Not sick at all," Mr. Ford continues. He sucks on his teeth. "Nope, I saw her at Superfood on 4th and Pine when I was waiting at the intersection. She had a cart full of food. Not sick at all, and shopping at a competitor."

"People still shop when they're sick," I say.

"Paper or plastic?" he asks the next customer. Then to me, he hisses, "She was right as rain. I don't suppose Mr. Sneezbee would be happy, regardless."

"Oh, come on," I say. "Stay out of it. Do you want her to get fired?"

He says nothing, just smirks at me.

I tell the customer, "You saved fifteen cents. Thanks for shopping here."

"Paper or plastic?" Mr. Ford asks the next customer.

I ring them through. "You saved some money," I tell them, distracted. I want to scream at Mr. Ford that he's an evil shit, but then it occurs to me that I've been thinking the same thing about myself.

I take a break instead. I walk outside, into sunlight that makes my eyeballs hurt. Bea sits there alone at the staff picnic table, eating a sandwich and flipping through a fashion magazine. I sit across from her. She looks at me, her eyes small and afraid.

She knows. She knows what we did.

I take a deep breath.

"Listen," I tell her, trying to sound as distant and adult as my dad once sounded. "I'm sorry. I am. But I can't be mad at myself for the things that I've done. Life is too short. You'll have to forgive me, too."

Bea puts down her sandwich. Her eyes bore into me, filled with pain and rage. Her anger is so familiar that I could reach out and stroke its head. I reacted the same way to those words. There is nothing left to do, then, but get up and leave. Like Dad did.

I don't, though. I just sit there like I'm made of wood. A plane roars overhead. Bea shuffles and coughs. *Wait*, I think. *Wait just a while longer. I'll say something beautiful. The perfect thing. Just wait.* She shoves the remains of her sandwich into a brown paper bag. She swings one of her heavy legs over the bench, straddling it.

To my relief, she goes still. To my relief, she waits.

I take a deep breath and start over.

The words are not beautiful or perfect, but I'm saying them, anyway.

VVVVVVVVVVVVVVVVVVVVVVV

THE WRITER'S WEREWOLF

∧∧∧∧∧∧∧∧∧∧∧∧∧∧∧∧∧∧∧∧∧∧∧∧

Chapter One: The Writer Meets the Werewolf

For most people who met the werewolf on a moonlit night, a bloodbath ensued. It might have been so for Nicky, too, but he was so self-absorbed that he hardly registered the bearlike frame in front of him, which gnashed its teeth and pummeled its breast, creating a general ruckus as was the werewolf's wont.

Nicky just stood there, downtrodden. "Dude. You want what's in my wallet or what?"

The werewolf slackened, retracting his claws and fangs. He seemed startled by Nicky's question.

"I just want you to react," the werewolf replied.

"Ha," Nicky said. The irony of it nearly killed him. "Well, give writing a shot. That will really depress you, man."

"I didn't mean to interrupt anything," the werewolf said apologetically. He was a little confused. "So you're a writer then?"

Nicky looked up and peered into his aggressor's face. "You a werewolf?"

They both sort of nodded for a moment, understanding one another.

"You wanna catch a beer, man?" Nicky asked. "I'd like to talk to someone about this story I'm writing."

They moved toward a bar, the tavern they would meet at monthly from this point forward.

As they walked, Nicky grappled for words. He was near tears. "It's not about the money, you know. I just want to *move* people. I want to write something *transportive.*"

The werewolf crept beside him, listening.

Chapter Two: Little Nicky, Before Werewolf

Nicky had three short story collections. Long ones. He thought of himself as a modern-day Chekhov. None of the books, however, were published. He lived off of his trust fund, staying up most hours of the night to type a minimum of two thousand words. It was a glorious, frustrating existence. "The best of times, the worst of times," he quoted. Then, grimacing, Nicky wondered why he couldn't pen such a fantastic intro, himself.

Almost daily he received rejections. Some were promising, some were negative. Most of them were indifferent. One day a publisher called and said they were interested. Nicky heartily expressed his gratitude. He waited impatiently for a contract that never came. He started calling daily to check in with them. And when, he asked in a strained tone, would they publish his book? The editors hemmed and hawed. Several weeks passed. Now they refused to take his calls.

"Is it worth it?" Nicky said to the mirror. His eyes were bloodshot, half-crazy.

"What a question," he replied, sighing. "It's all worth it."

His mother left long messages on his answering machine. "I was at the grocery store today," she would say, "and the woman ahead of me was talking on her cell phone, completely ignoring the grocery clerk, who kept asking his co-worker what the price of grapes was, and the line was, like, really long, and I was feeling so frustrated about it that I almost set my grocery basket on the floor and walked out! I didn't do that, of course, but later, as I was telling your father the story, I threw up my hands and laughed and said, 'Wouldn't this be an amazing thing for Little Nicky to write about?'"

With a roll of his eyes Nicky would hit the delete button and plunge back into his manuscripts.

Chapter Three: The Werewolf's New Career

Sometimes the werewolf wondered if he ever really was a normal guy. Nicky said he had to be, that was the way with werewolves, but the werewolf felt as though he had been alive since the dawn of time, that it had always been nightfall, that the sky had always been clear and the moon full. Couldn't it be true?

One night Nicky showed him a photograph of a sunny beach. There was a red and white beach ball, a long-stemmed umbrella; there was pale sand and gently breaking waves. In the foreground, a beautiful woman wearing a tiny bikini sunned her hairless body so that it shone like starlight.

"Wow," the werewolf said. "Where is that?"

"Thailand," Nicky replied. "You can't go there. You're a werewolf."

The werewolf was crushed and almost insulted. But he knew Nicky didn't mean it. After all, he was a just a normal guy. A thin, pasty, balding normal guy, a guy who hid his age by wearing a baseball cap. It would be hard to get the werewolf thing if that was all you knew.

When you're friends with someone, you forgive certain things. The werewolf had kept few friends since the dawn of time, and Nicky would be dead soon while he kept living. So he embraced their friendship – however flawed, however one-sided – with all of his furry might.

He was proud of Nicky. He had never known a writer before and it amazed him the sheer volume his friend had written.

So when Nicky gave him the first manuscript to read, the werewolf was truly impressed. It needed some work, sure. It was a little rough around the edges. The werewolf humbly gave some advice.

Nicky was hurt. "You didn't like it."

"No, I really liked it, Nicky. I'm just trying to help. Perhaps a couple of these stories could be changed from the 'I' to the 'he/she' perspective."

"It's called third-person," Nicky said dully. He folded his arms across his chest and scowled.

"Okay, then, third-person. See? I don't know what I'm talking about. I know nothing about writing. I only know about howling at the moon, about fleas."

Nicky shook his head and a steely determination crossed his face. "No. No. This is good. I need this. I'm sorry. Please, continue. Third-person you say? What will that accomplish?"

"Since all twenty stories are taking place in an apartment, it might vary the stories up a bit. You know, the perspective change."

Nicky nodded, slowly at first, then more and more energetically. "Okay," he said. "Okay. This is good stuff. Keep it coming." He unfolded his arms and leaned forward. "This is solid gold."

The werewolf was relieved. For the first time since the dawn of time, his opinion was invited.

Chapter Four: The Writer Wishes to Express His Gratitude

The werewolf was now instrumental in his writing. Nicky cursed a blue streak when clouds kept the moon concealed, a fate that happened far too often in Seattle. Nonetheless, the hard work paid off. After nearly two years of meetings with his monstrous friend, a small independent press finally agreed to publish his first short-story collection. It was, for Nicky, a dream come true.

Nicky fantasized about the cover. An apartment with no furniture, perhaps? Or a simple illustration of a heart on the floor? That would be jarring. He fantasized about the type font. Could he create his own? Could he call it Georgian Classic Chant X font? Or Goblet Bold? Something archaic?

That would be awesome.

He also fantasized about the intro. "To Grandpa, thanks for the trust fund." No, scratch that. "To Grandpa, thanks for the support. To Mom and Dad, thanks for all of the inspiration over the years." But he would save the best for last, the best for his best friend: "To the Werewolf. This collection would never have seen the light of day (haha!) without you. You're my best editor, my best friend. Here's to you on my big day!" Scratch that. "Here's to you on *our* big day!"

Under all that dark hair, the werewolf would be tickled pink.

Chapter Five: The Celebration, Ruined

At the bar, Nicky unveiled the big news. "Read this," he told the werewolf.

The werewolf unfolded the letter carefully, trying not to tear the paper with his large claws. He mumbled to himself as he read, his dark hairy face gradually brightening.

"Well by gum, Nicky, you've really done it!"

"I'm just so damn happy. You know, they don't pay very much, but the prestige of this independent is well-known. I'm a lucky fellow."

"Not luck," the werewolf said, smiling, handing the letter back to him. "It's talent. Pure, unfiltered talent."

"My friend, we both know I couldn't have done this without you."

"I'm so happy for you, Nicky. You know I am."

Nicky looked at the werewolf. There were tears in both of their eyes. The werewolf was truly happy for him, and Nicky could see it.

"Let's get some beer to celebrate."

The werewolf agreed.

After they clinked beer bottles, the werewolf took a swig and then unbuttoned his flannel shirt.

"Whoa, turbo," Nicky joked. "I don't need a stripper tonight. And I prefer hairless female ones at that."

The werewolf laughed. He pulled out a manuscript and set it on the table, re-buttoning his shirt.

"I'm in a good mood, too," he said.

"What's that?" Nicky asked, his smile fading slightly as he eyed the thick pile of paper.

"I've been tinkering a little bit," the werewolf said shyly. He touched the manuscript. "It's a novel. About being a werewolf. You know, the hardships."

"You've been writing?"

"Yeah. I thought I'd surprise you when I was finished."

Nicky's mouth had gone dry. He fingered the thin envelope, his acceptance letter, in his coat pocket. It was hot to the touch.

"Wow," Nicky said. "Wow. I had no idea."

"You said when we first met that it was a great way to get a reaction out of people. That always stuck with me." The werewolf noticed Nicky's nervous fingers and stricken look. "Of course, it's nothing like yours. It's not as good as your writing."

"Well, of course," Nicky sputtered. He calmed himself down. It couldn't be good, he thought hurriedly to himself, I mean, werewolves can't write. Right? "Of course I'll read it, I mean. Of course I will. I can't wait."

He tried to finish his beer and remain buoyant, but his big night had been ruined.

Chapter Six: Role Reversal

At home, drunk, Nicky opened up the manuscript and pored through it from top to bottom. Amazing. Nuanced. Complicated and yet so simple. *The writing is not Chekhov,* Nicky realized. *It's all his own. It's worldly. It's enormous. It's perfect. It's haunting. It's everything my writing is not.*

Nicky finished reading, sober now and destroyed. He curled himself up into a ball and wept. He wrapped his fists around his skull and screamed into his knees. He tore out small bits of hair and the ache made him cry harder. Goddamn it, he thought. How could his friend undermine him like this? Didn't he understand that Nicky had been working for this his entire life? What gave him the right to swoop in – *a writing virgin,* for crissakes – and overtake Nicky's dream? It was diabolical. Nicky wanted to die.

Overcome, he threw open the window. He leaned out and howled. Passersby on the street below clucked their tongues. *He's drunk,* they muttered. *On drugs.* Another person, someone with more imagination, thought it sounded like a wolf's howl.

The sun was just beginning to set. The werewolf would not appear for another month.

Chapter Seven: The Battery

At the bar, the werewolf studied Nicky carefully. "Are you okay?"

Nicky was half-asleep at the table. He had accomplished nothing over the past few weeks, whiling away his waking hours with torturous re-readings of the werewolf's novel. He had barely eaten, he had barely slept. A box of Nicky's recently published books sat crammed under the bed, unopened.

"I'm fine," he said. "Tired. Busy."

"You probably didn't get a chance to look over my novel then?"

Nicky opened up a manila folder and pulled out the manuscript. He deposited it in front of the werewolf. His eyes were distant and strange. They had a cruel glitter to them that the werewolf mistook as indifference.

The manuscript was intensely battered. It was battered from Nicky weeping on it and hugging it to his body in his sleep. But when the werewolf opened it up there were vicious slashes of red marker on almost every line. The werewolf, stunned, was reminded of the claw marks he would leave on his victims, claw marks he hadn't made since he'd taken up writing.

"It was okay," Nicky said hollowly. His voice was insincere.

"You really worked on this, didn't you?" The werewolf was staring at the pages, overwhelmed by all of the corrections. "Oh my God."

"It's all a part of writing," Nicky said. "Welcome to the real world, my friend."

"I'm so embarrassed."

"Don't be. We all have to start somewhere."

The werewolf was taking it pretty hard. Watching him, Nicky winced. The werewolf's strong broad shoulders sank lower with every page he turned. Nicky's stomach grew queasy. He pinched himself in the leg, angrily.

"Don't worry about it," he repeated, "we all have to start somewhere."

Nicky watched the werewolf fold the novel back into his flannel shirt. He was withdrawn and humiliated.

"You just have to work on it some more, man."

The werewolf tried to force a smile and failed. "I might return to the streets early tonight."

"Let's have some beers first."

The werewolf shrugged. "This writing stuff is hard. I don't think I have the heart for it."

Nicky knew what he should say.

It's the best I've ever read.

I love it.

You have it, and I don't.

Don't give up, man, you can be more than just a werewolf.

Nicky's gut churned. "Jesus Christ," he blurted out, "can you please button up your shirt? People are staring. There's fucking hair everywhere."

The werewolf rubbed at his eyes. He was too heartbroken to respond.

Later, a bloodbath. The werewolf would get the reaction he wanted from some stranger in the street. He would lift them into the air as they flailed and wept. He would tear the limbs from their torso. All of the words and peace that had filled his soul would crack.

"Have mercy! Please God have mercy!"

And he would not.

vvvvvvvvvvvvvvvvvvvvvvvvv

THE ONES

ΛΛΛΛΛΛΛΛΛΛΛΛΛΛΛΛΛΛΛΛΛΛΛΛΛ

In junior high I shared my first kiss with the boy who wore a pro-phetic glass eyeball. In high school I lost my virginity to the wolfman, whose face was like the back of my head, entirely covered in hair. In col-lege I was briefly engaged to the moodier half of Siamese twins, but he was perennially jealous of his attached brother. I ended the relationship one Saturday morning after they came to blows. In my thirties I met a man named Kurt, a middle-aged denture-wearer. Fake teeth were not a prob-lem. This was relatively normal given my dating history, and I watched with a sort of sick fascination when he popped out his teeth before sliding into bed with me. I wondered that first night if he could be The One. He might have been, if his dentures hadn't been able to speak.

I discovered this in Manito Park while we lounged in the flower gar-den's stone gazebo. All of the tops of the flowers had been chopped off in preparation for winter, and the remaining stems were like bareheaded anorexics swaying drunkenly in the breeze. My boyfriend was talking about *Anna Karenina*, about how much more fully realized of a novel it was compared to *War and Peace*, the sort of inane, blusterous getting-to-know-you conversations that pepper the start of a new relationship. I had enjoyed both books and had never tried to decide which was better – to do so was rather unfair, I privately surmised – but I found his speech thrilling. Few of my other boyfriends could be classified as intellectuals. I smelled a real catch here.

Then, out of nowhere, someone began to argue with my boyfriend.

"What a joke," the voice said. "*Anna Karenina* can't hold a candle to *War and Peace*. I mean come on. You've got that terrific bore Levin and that terrific melodramatic boob Anna. What a pair of assholes! Compare those sniveling morons to the fully realized Prince Andrei, or to Pierre, or to Nata-sha. There's no contest."

I had been leaning back on my elbows against the short marble wall of the gazebo. Now I sat up in surprise, glancing around at our surround-ings. There was no one near us.

"The ending to *War and Peace* is so very tedious," my boyfriend was saying.

"Oh, smelly *balls*," the voice said, clearly annoyed. "Granted, that chapter blows. But it only makes the rest of the book more luminous in comparison."

The voice was opinionated, but muted. Somewhat tinny. I realized with a terrible sinking feeling that it was coming from my boyfriend's head. The dentures shimmied in his mouth, alive. The voice continued, "When Anna threw herself under the train, I was like, *Finally. Thank God.*"

The dentures. The dentures were speaking. Not only speaking, but opining. What unfortunate luck I had with men, I lamented inwardly. For once I get a decently normal boyfriend, but now these strange talking dentures!

This reminded me of an event, years ago, when my first-kiss had held his prophetic glass eyeball in his palm and read me my future. "Normally wine comes in at the mouth," he had said, " and love comes in at the eye. But for you, love comes in at the mouth." At the time, I thought it was a pretty good line to get us to kiss. But maybe it had more portent than I originally assumed. Perhaps he meant with Kurt, more specifically with Kurt's strange mouth, this vessel of magical dentures. I struggled to be open-minded, but could feel myself failing.

"What kind of books do you like?" my boyfriend said, shifting toward me. He smiled, fully engaged. The dentures winked at me in the sunlight.

Kurt noticed then how white I had gone, how closely I was watching his mouth. He put up a hand and shielded the dentures from my sight.

"They…" I gestured vaguely and he nodded.

"I know, I know." He lowered his hand and looked away. "Are they bothering you? They bother most women."

"Give him a chance," the dentures called from their moist cavern. "He's really a swell guy!"

Despite their disagreements over literature (and movies and music and all other things, as I later found out), the dentures and their owner were clearly fond of one another.

And it occurred to me that I was being unfair. Were talking dentures so far different from a prophetic eyeball, from a hairy face? I was not the sort of woman who ran away screaming from such a commitment. Compassion bloomed like love in me. I reached over and took my boyfriend's clammy hand in mine and squeezed it.

"No," I said. "It's fine. Really, it's not a problem."

As we walked back through the park, I told him about some of my ex-boyfriends. "I'm accustomed to weirdness. Trust me."

He put his arms around me and kissed me between my eyes. A small cold circle remained there after he pulled away. We held hands all the way to the car. By the time we parked in his driveway, I was convinced that I had found The One.

That night I was overcome by restlessness, as I frequently was in those days. I went to the bathroom to floss my teeth and to stare glassily into the mirror. It was a way to soothe myself. There were my boyfriend's dentures, smiling up at me from their grimy brown aquarium, an old coffee mug that read, *If it ain't broke, don't fix it.*

"How's it going?" they said.

I bared my teeth to the mirror and with my tongue dislodged a fleck of pepper from the sharp edge of an incisor. "Fine," I said. It was surprisingly easy to start a conversation with a pair of dentures. They seemed so vulnerable. "How is it," I asked, "that a forty-year-old has no teeth?"

"Boxing," the dentures replied. "Hasn't he told you? He was a featherweight in Mexico. He won, you know. But following the match his opponent's gang attacked him in the street. They kicked out his teeth."

This seemed satisfactory, brave to say the least. I had never before dated someone brave. I worried that this lowered my status with him.

"That's when I came into the picture," the dentures continued proudly. "I've been really lucky. He's a good guy."

The dentures, perhaps noticing my worried expression, blew bubbles in the water to get my attention.

"Hey there," they warbled cheerfully. "You're a wonderful kisser, you know. He really likes you. I can tell."

"You're not so bad, yourself," I said, relaxing. I recalled licking the front of these dentures – unwittingly, of course – as recently as the night before. They had been clean and smooth, making me self-conscious of my own crooked teeth, which were damaged from years of anxious gritting.

"Sleep tight," the dentures said as I turned out the light. "See you tomorrow."

I snuck back in bed and kissed my boyfriend's crumpled face. If this was his only flaw, his only secret, then I, too, was lucky. His eyelids slowly scrolled open. When he saw me, he smiled. I stroked the curly hairs on his chest.

"I had a great conversation with your dentures," I confessed lightheartedly.

"Oh uh," he said, sitting up.

"No, seriously. They're great. I like them a lot."

He wrapped his arms around me and I rested my head on the crook of his armpit. His smell was musky and sweet. "You're really amazing," he said. Without his teeth, he lisped.

Kurt and I spent a blissful few weeks together. We hiked in Riverside Park and rode the carousel. He drove me around in his paint-chipped maroon Buick, an old car whose interior he kept sparkling clean. On the weekends he took me out for cocktails at dive bars on Sprague that I'd never set foot in alone, bars with bartenders older than stone, and ordered me ice-cold drinks like whiskey and sodas or dry martinis with a twist. For himself he would request a can of lukewarm beer; cold beverages hurt his sensitive gums. I said silly charming things to make him smile. When his mouth cracked open I admired his dentures. They gazed back at me, gleaming.

As my intimacy deepened with Kurt, so did my intimacy with his dentures. The three of us would hold erudite discussions for hours on all sorts of varied subjects. Sometimes the two of them would be chattering to me about different subjects at the same time – as though competing with one another for my attention – and I would have to scream at them, "Shut up," so I could hear myself think. Even when I wanted to speak to Kurt alone, the dentures would venture their unsought opinion. Despite this annoying situation, or perhaps because of it, my bond with the dentures deepened. As the months passed I found myself going to the bathroom more and more frequently. I kept our clandestine midnight chats a secret. Kurt snored softly in the bedroom, unaware.

Eventually the dentures professed their love for me.

I was leaning against the sink on my elbows, my face looming over the coffee mug.

"Don't say such things!" I cried passionately. "I'm with Kurt. This is my chance for real love. You're wrecking it."

"You don't love Kurt. You love what's damaged about Kurt. You love me. I can tell when you're talking to him. Your eyes glaze over. He's too perfect, too boring. But you and me, we're both crutches. We're both alien. We relate. Why, you're even more intimate with me. You don't even pee in front of Kurt! Don't you see?"

"Stop," I said, but my knees were weak. "Please stop."

It didn't help that the teeth were Kurt's best feature. They glittered like diamonds when Kurt grinned. My stomach began to twirl whenever I saw them. Perhaps, at first, some of the attraction was the forbiddance of it. The dentures knew they were getting to me. One night, overcome, I lifted them into the palm of my hand and pressed my lips against them. It was the first time we had touched without Kurt in between us.

"My love," the dentures said huskily, "my life, my passion. Take me away from here. Steal me away. No more lies."

I went back to the bedroom and stuffed the dentures into my purse. I dressed silently, keeping a wary eye on the bed. Kurt could sleep through a train wreck, and so he slept now. He was the best guy I'd ever dated, and I worried that he would be crushed. I left him a note, "I'm sorry. It's over. You are an amazing guy, though, and I wish you the best." It was shitty note, but it would have to do. I placed it on my pillow, so that he would read it first thing when he awoke. Then I tiptoed out of his apartment, expecting never to see him again.

He phoned me the next morning, fuming. "You break my heart and *steal my teeth*?"

"I wanted something to remember you by," I lied. The dentures sighed audibly.

"I'm coming straight over there to get them."

I protested vehemently. He could come, but I would never relinquish them.

"They cost me $900 per arch!"

"Okay then," I said. "I'll pay you."

He was weeping now. "I thought you were The One. I wanted to marry you. Is there someone else?"

I remained silent.

"There's someone else," he moaned. "God!"

"It's not what you think," I told him. I cradled the dentures in my palm. They were solid and light at the same time. "But it's true: I'm moving on."

He heaved a heart-rending sob and then hung up. I took out my checkbook and wrote out a check for $1800. I sent it that very day. Kurt never cashed it, which didn't help with the guilt factor. But it was over. Our relationship was finished, and the dentures and I were together, blissfully unhindered.

A year or so later I was in the grocery store when I ran into Kurt. A pretty woman hung daintily from his arm like fine jewelry. She seemed very attached. I wondered if she knew about his teeth, or lack thereof. He had new dentures, but they were nothing like his old ones.

I smiled at him. "Hello, Kurt," I said. "It's good to see you."

He smiled at me in a friendly, sincere way and murmured his own greeting. He introduced me to his girlfriend. We chatted shallowly for a few minutes, curious about one another, but too timid to ask probing questions. He was studying my face carefully. He pulled back all of a sudden, mid-sentence, and brought a hand to his mouth.

"Your teeth…" he said.

My gaze fell to the floor. I stopped smiling. "Yes," I said.

"Those are my old – "

"Yes," I confirmed, nodding, "they are." I gathered whatever courage I had and looked him directly in the eyes. "It was what we wanted."

"But what about your other teeth?" He was horror-stricken. His girlfriend watched us, her delicate brow furrowing in confusion.

I shook my head. "It was nothing," I said.

"The pain you must have endured," Kurt added sympathetically. "My God. Well." He grimaced for a moment, perhaps recollecting a past agony. "I hope you're happy. Sincerely, I do."

It had indeed been painful. I nodded, paling at the memory. But I had not suffered alone. The dentures, too, had been shaven down, reshaped. Now we were together always. Such was the way with relationships. Pain was a necessary ingredient.

We said our goodbyes then and earnestly wished one another the best. I watched Kurt and his girlfriend loop away from us, winding through the colorful baskets of fruits and vegetables.

"Holy crap," I said.

"That wasn't as awkward as we feared," the dentures mused. "I'm glad it's over."

"You know," I said wistfully, "he's a good guy."

"Yeah. He always was."

We purchased our groceries and went out into the parking lot. We were looking forward to an evening alone.

It had rained recently and there were worms everywhere, gumming forlornly at the rough pavement. They had escaped during the flood and were now lost. They searched clumsily for the soil, and some would find it, but many others would perish, fried by the pitiless sun into crispy brown husks. Those poor worms, I thought, gazing down at the squirming tubes of their bodies. They were so blind. So unlucky.

And me, so far above them.

So happy.

So in love.

THE AUTUMN HOUSE FICTION SERIES

New World Order by Derek Green
Drift and Swerve by Samuel Ligon ▲ 2008
Monongahela Dusk by John Hoerr
Attention Please Now by Matthew Pitt ▲ 2009
Peter Never Came by Ashley Cowger ▲ 2010
*Keeping the Wolves at Bay: Stories by Emerging
   American Writers*, Sharon Dilworth, ed.
Party Girls by Diane Goodman
Favorite Monster by Sharma Shields ▲ 2011

▲ Winners of the Autumn House Fiction Prize

vvvvvvvvvvvvvvvvvvvvvvvvv

DESIGN AND PRODUCTION

ΛΛΛΛΛΛΛΛΛΛΛΛΛΛΛΛΛΛΛΛΛΛΛΛΛ

Cover and text design by Kathy Boykowycz

Text set in Myriad, designed in 1991 by Robert Slimbach and Carol Twombly; titles set in Spumoni, designed in 1990 by Garrett Boge

Printed by McNaughton & Gunn, Saline, Michigan, on Nature's Book, a 30% recycled paper